Special thanks to:

Amanda Kay Smith, Anij Fallows, Azia MacManus, Burning Spear Comix, Carl W Bishop, Catherine Leja, Chris Call, Christine Gourley, Collin David, Courtney Cannon, Damion and Cathy Gilzean, Daniel Groves, Dave Baxter, DeWayne Copeland, Earl Hall, Elizabeth Nohelty Romano, Emerson Kasak, Erin Congdon, Jake Schroeder, Jason Crase, Jeff Lewis, Jimbo, John Mead, Joshua Bowers, Katrina Roets, Ken Reich, Kimberly Lucia, Laura Reed, Mark Byzewski, Mark Hill, Massimo Piras, Matthew Johnson, Michael H Bullington, Nick Smith, Nikres, Odile Purcell O'Byrne, Paul Rose Jr., Peter Anders, Rob Fowler, Rob Steinberger, Sammy G., scantrontb, Schreuka, Scott Kilburn, Shannon Carlin, Sherry Mock, SwordFirey, Talinda Willard, Thomas Werner, Venron, and Walter Weiss.

ALSO BY RUSSELL NOHELTY

THE GODVERSE CHRONICLES
And Death Followed Behind Her
And Doom Followed Behind Her
And Ruin Followed Behind Her
And Hell Followed Behind Her
Katrina Hates the Dead
Pixie Dust

OTHER NOVEL WORK
My Father Didn't Kill Himself
Sorry for Existing
Gumshoes: The Case of Madison's Father
Invasion
The Vessel
Worst Thing in the Universe
The Marked Ones

OTHER ILLUSTRATED WORK
The Little Bird and the Little Worm
Ichabod Jones: Monster Hunter
Gherkin Boy

www.russellnohelty.com

The Void Calls Us Home

By:

Russell Nohelty

Edited by:

Leah Lederman

Proofread by:

Katrina Roets

Cover by:
Paramita Bhattacharjee

Rebecca,

I can't do this anymore. I tried everything. The call is too great. It's too strong. It hounds me at all hours of the day and night. It consumes my every waking thought.

It will never let me go.

I have tried to deny it. I have tried to drown it out, but it is too much. It calls me to it. It calls me home. I must heed the call and return to the Void. I love you so much.

Goodbye.

Mary

Chapter 1

I have never been suicidal.

Sure, I've had dark thoughts in my life, but who hasn't? They were never more than just a passing thought that swooped into my mind and left as quickly as they came. I was a relatively happy human female, all things considered, and yet…

I think I tried to kill myself last night. I hate using the word "think". I mean, if I tried to kill myself, that's the kind of thing I should know, right?

It is, but that didn't change the fact I just wasn't sure.

God, that sounded so moronic. Even stupider than it sounded rattling around in my brain. It's just that, one moment, I was driving along, minding my own business. And then, I was off the side of the road, plummeting down an embankment, and slamming into a tree. The rest of the car ride I remembered vividly, but that last moment...

The reason that I jerked the wheel to the right on that lonely, dark, mountain road…that's what was fuzzy.

I remembered singing along to Kesha's "Rainbow", where she goes, "I've found a rainbow, rainbow, baby Trust me, I know, life is scary, but just put those colors on, girl. Come and play along with me tonight…" Suddenly the temperature in my car plummeted. The hair on my arms stood up on end and I felt as if my insides were being hollowed out, as if every good thought in my body had been stripped away from me.

I stopped singing. I stopped everything and stared blankly out into the dark night. It was rainy, and the thick drops fell onto my windshield. The wipers whipped across the glass as they struggled to keep the water at bay. I should have replaced them months ago, but it always slipped my mind.

The music must have still been on right before the car jerked to the right, but I couldn't hear it anymore. All I heard was the rhythmic wiping of the windshield as I peered out into the dark beyond my headlights. The darkness hypnotized me. Hopelessness washed over me, utter hopelessness; despair that felt eternal.

Then, I spun my wheel to the right...

...and I fell...

When my head slammed into the steering wheel, the darkness engulfed me. I drifted through the nothing like some dark, underwater pit, except that I wasn't drowning. I wasn't gasping for breath. I wasn't even frightened. I was one with the black. Without hope, fear, or happiness. I just...was.

I heard the muffled sounds of the medics prying me from the car, and later the voices of doctors as they worked to save my life, but I couldn't see them. I couldn't feel them. I was numb, completely and utterly without feeling, left with nothing but the frigid cold.

I don't know how long I floated in the emptiness. I swam in every direction, looking for a flicker of warmth that eluded me. I longed for comfort, for heat, for answers, but no matter how far I travelled, there was nothing around me. I screamed into the abyss, but there was nobody there.

Without warning, a great force jerked me by the throat and pulled me out of the darkness. I woke up gasping for breath. My eyes fluttered opened, and I sucked in oxygen as if I had come back from drowning.

Nurses and doctors flooded into the room as I spasmed uncontrollably on the bed, kicking off the fresh linens. A needle jabbed in my arm, and then, it was quiet again. This time, I did not fall into the hopeless void, but into a pleasant dream, where I was a pony.

The second time I woke, my eyes focused on my mother. She looked as though she hadn't slept in days. Her short, blonde hair was tangled, and her face was greasy. Dark circles rested under her eyes. I hadn't seen her without make-up once in my entire life, and the sight was enough to jar me awake.

"Mom?" I asked, weakly. I tried to push myself to my elbows, but the pain in my chest burned and I collapsed back onto the hospital bed like a ten-ton rock.

"Becca!" Mom said, her voice cracking with excitement. "Becca! You're awake!"

She jumped up and wrapped her arms around my neck. She pressed herself closely and my chest throbbed again.

"Ow," I said to her. My mother was not an emotional person by any stretch of the imagination. I couldn't remember her ever hugging me like that, and yet she held me so tight I thought I would burst.

"Sorry," Mom said, pushing herself back and wiping the tears from her eyes. "I didn't know if I would ever see you again."

"It's okay," I said, taking a deep heave of air. Every breath was agony, but I couldn't stop taking long inhales and exhales, enjoying my breath in a way I never had before. "How long have I been…how long have I been out?"

"Four weeks," she replied. "They told me you would never wake up, but I knew. I just knew that you would. I…knew."

Mom swallowed her sadness as the tears came again. Mom hadn't even cried at my sister's funeral, and yet here she was, sobbing at my bedside. She tried to talk but it was no use. All that eked out where mumbled syllables that I couldn't understand. She collapsed back onto the chair and wept into her hands.

"You're up!" I heard from the doorway.

I turned my aching head to see my father standing at the door with two cups of coffee. He was a big man, and broad. He could have played linebacker in the NFL with his massive size, except that he had the coordination of a running camel.

"Hi, Dad," I replied, groggy. "Ignore Mom. She's having a moment."

Dad smiled at me. "She's emotional, kiddo."

"I know," I said. "I don't know what to do. This is a foreign experience to me."

"Just give her a minute."

He barreled forward to give me a hug, but I held out my hand to stop him. My arms throbbed as they swung above my body.

"Please, no," I said. "I don't think my body can take one of your bear hugs right now."

He shrugged, disappointed but understanding. My father was not emotionally stilted like my mother. He was responsible for most of the affection I received in my life. My sister accounted for the rest, but…

"I get it," he said, holding up his hand. "I'm just, oh, I'm really glad to see you, is all." He leaned forward to place a gentle kiss on my forehead.

My vision swirled and crackled, and my eyes turned up into my head. I tried to keep my head up, but it was no use. I collapsed back in bed and drifted off, hoping I would dream of kittens and not the black nothingness I had been trapped in for so long.

Chapter 2

I drifted in and out of consciousness for the next three days. When I was awake, the pain was excruciating, but being asleep was even worse. When I was asleep, I was haunted by an image.

It was a thousand-foot-high black eye, sucking blue and orange flames into itself from every direction. It searched for me in the darkness, but it could not find me, no matter where it looked. I waved my arms, desperate for it to see me, but it did not. It was a nightmare, not because it searched for me, but because it couldn't find me.

I wanted desperately for the flaming eye to see me. I called out to it, begging for its warmth to save me from the cold darkness, but when it turned to my direction, it only looked through me, no matter how much I screamed and flailed my arms.

I might have chalked up my recurring dreams to just that, crazy dreams, if I wasn't remembering more about my crash with each passing day.

That flaming eye…

I had seen it before. I didn't remember it when I first woke up, but the longer I was awake, the more I remembered…

It had flashed in front of my eyes the moment before I jerked my car off the road. It was the reason I swerved off the mountain in the first place. It had beckoned me toward it, and I desperately wanted to answer the call. After I slipped into a coma, I searched for it in the darkness. It was my salvation, and yet, it had abandoned me.

I didn't know I why wanted the flaming eye to take me away. I led a good life, a charmed life even; a life that I loved. I went to a great school, lived in a beautiful house, and already had three offers to Ivy League schools in my junior year of high school.

I'm privileged. Not everybody got the chance to play on the varsity basketball team, and even few could still pull straight A's while doing it. I wasn't trying to brag, mind you, just explaining that I totally understand how lucky I was. Depression couldn't have been the reason I pulled my car off the road. I wasn't depressed.

"Good afternoon, Ms. Rose." A short, squat doctor with frizzy, red hair walked into my room. "I'm Doctor Montrell. How are you doing this afternoon?"

"Fine, doctor," I lied.

"Don't sound too confident," Doctor Montrell replied. "I mean, you're alive. That must account for something, and conscious, which in and of itself is a bit of a miracle."

"I'm in a lot of pain," I said. "But I'm trying to keep a stiff upper lip about it. Still sucks though."

"Yeah, it does, and it's okay to think your situation sucks," Doctor Montrell said. She was flipping through pages on my chart. "I mean, you really hurt yourself. It's okay to admit that to me, all right. I need to know the truth. Understand?"

I hung my head. "Yes, doctor."

"Good. Now is there anything you need to tell me?"

"No, doctor."

"You don't sound too confident."

I wasn't confident. I wanted more than anything to tell somebody about the flaming eye in my dreams and figure out why I wanted to kill myself and join it. I'm young, bright, and generally positive, most of the time. Some people might even call me a ball of freaking sunshine, and yet…I had tried to kill myself.

But I couldn't tell her anything, could I? Not yet. At least not without having my sanity questioned. I needed to get out of the hospital first, and then maybe I could find some answers.

"My head just hurts a lot," I said.

"Well, that's normal after suffering a severe concussion. You'll feel better with time."

"Thanks," I replied. "Hey, Doc. When am I gonna be able to go home?"

"Let's get you up and walking around, and then we'll see about sending you home, okay?"

I smiled, even though it hurt my bruised cheeks. "Okay."

"Your physical therapist will be in shortly," Doctor Montrell said, walking toward the door. "Be honest with her about your pain levels, okay? Don't try to push yourself. She holds your future in her hands. You don't leave until she says it's okay."

The doctor left, and I fell back into bed, trembling in pain. Even with the painkillers, I still felt the sting in my chest every time I moved.

I tried to remember how lucky I was. It could have been much worse. I broke my arm, bruised three ribs, and snapped my nose when I slammed my head into the steering wheel, but I wasn't dead. By all accounts, I should have been.

Chapter 3

I'm no stranger to working out. I played a lot of sports, and that meant I focused on physical fitness. Basketball was my favorite sport, but in the off-season I was a sprinter on the track team. Coaches said I had an explosive first step.

I spent a lot of time in the woods, running alone to build up my endurance. When I wasn't running, I lifted weights.

I was in good shape, which made it all the more maddening when I couldn't even lift a five-pound weight during my first physical therapy session.

"That's normal after a big trauma," my physical therapist, Jill, told me. Her smile was wide enough that I wanted to punch it. "You're doing great." She picked up the three-pound weight and placed it into my hand. "Try this one."

"No," I replied. "I can do the five pounds, just give me a little more—"

"Hey," Jill said, grabbing my wrist gently. "You don't have to prove anything to me."

"Sure I do." I grimaced from the weight. "I have to prove I'm ready to go home."

"And you're not going to do that by pushing yourself past your limit. I'm trying to make sure you don't hurt yourself by doing too much too fast."

I used my non-broken arm to wipe the sweat from my forehead. "I'm sorry."

"It's not your fault. Everybody's like that after a big injury. Look over there."

Jill pointed across the gym at a woman in a wheelchair. Her jaw was slack, and her eyes were glazed over as if her brain was somewhere else. A plump man without any hair pulled her up to her feet and helped her to a set of parallel bars.

"Six months ago, she was walking and talking up a storm. Then, she had…well, she had an accident and now she can't do any of that anymore."

"Sad," I said.

"Not just sad, but frustrating for her, right? I mean, look at her. Do you think she wants to learn to walk again? She has to start at the beginning, as if she were a baby."

"Yeah, that sucks." I wasn't seeing her point.

Jill turned to me. "What I'm saying is that you don't have to start at the beginning, kiddo, but we all have to start somewhere. Is it fair? No, but neither is life."

The woman on the parallel bars took a step forward and wobbled, shaking on her feet until she collapsed into her therapist's arms. Instead of crying or yelling, she waited for her therapist to stand her up, and she tried again. I understood Jill's point, but there was a big difference between that woman and me. I had brought my pain on myself, and she hadn't. That made us very different.

Still, we were the same in that neither of us could take our mobility for granted. We had to actively work to get back to where we wanted to be, so I took the three-pound weight and clenched it in my hand. Struggling, I pulled that weight up to my chest, and let out a big breath of relief.

"Very good," Jill said. "That was hard, right?"

"So hard."

"It gets easier," Jill said. "You just have to work at it."

I pulled the weight up to my chest a second time. "I can do that. So, does that mean I can go home?"

She smiled. "I'll see what I can do."

One weird thing about hospitals was that they never wanted you to walk anywhere. Whenever I left my room, they insisted on wheeling me to every exam and appointment as if I were an invalid.

"Why can't I walk to my room?" I asked Jill as she wheeled me back to my hospital bed. "I have two perfectly good legs."

"Well," Jill said, "if you could just walk everywhere, then how would we have these wonderful little conversations, huh?"

"True, but if that's what it takes to talk to you, I could absolutely go without these little conversations. Like, without question, I could go without them. For sure."

"That hurts my feelings," Jill said, pushing me into my room.

"Well, that's not my intention," I said. "So, I'm stuck in this stupid wheelchair for a little while longer."

"Just a bit," Jill said. "You did a good job today. I'm going to tell the doctor and see what I can do to get you out of here and out of this wheelchair, okay?"

"Thanks," I replied with a smile.

Jill helped me out of my wheelchair, and I laid down on the bed. There wasn't much to do in a hospital when there weren't tests to run or homework to catch up on, so I spent a lot of time watching *Judge Judy* while laying on my back. It was mind-numbingly boring.

Luckily, I wasn't often alone for long lengths of time. Every day my best friend Tracy brought my homework from school and sat with me as I caught up on the gossip of the day.

Tracy lived for gossip. She was plugged into every clique at school, so she knew everything that was going on with everybody. I liked to sit back and listen as she filled me in on the day's events.

"Mark and Fran broke up," she told me in the middle of correcting my trigonometry homework. "Out of the blue."

"I didn't know they were together," I said.

"Oh, yeah, well it happened while you were asleep, and I just didn't have the heart to tell you he was seeing somebody."

Mark was my ex-boyfriend from eighth grade. Sorta. We only went on one date, but back then one date was enough. I did not think about him, ever, except when I saw him in the halls of school, and even then, it was barely for a fleeting second. Still, Tracy never saw a boy she didn't love madly, and she couldn't understand that I didn't feel the same way.

"I don't really care," I said.

"Oh, I know. I just thought, you know, any bad news could derail your progress. Besides, I figured their relationship wouldn't last. People only date Franny for one thing, you know?"

"I know what they say, for sure, but she doesn't seem like the slutty type to me."

"Well, I'm surprised. Frankly, compared to you everybody is a slut."

"That's not true!" I balled up a sheet of notebook paper and threw it at her.

"Really?" Tracy said. "And do you know why I keep bringing up Mark, then?"

"Because you can't get over the fact that I don't like him?"

"No," she said. "Because you haven't been on a date since him, so there's nothing else to talk about with you. Girl, you are the anti-gossip. It's amazing I'm friends with you."

I smiled. "I like to think I'm your palette cleanser in a world full of juicy and lurid relationships."

"That's true. You are like my plain yogurt."

Nobody could make me laugh like Tracy, which was usually a blessing but definitely a curse right now, when my ribs burned like fire every time I chuckled. However, it was worth it to feel normal again, even if it was just for a little while.

"Good news," Doctor Montrell said, walking into the room.

"Please tell me I'm going home."

She smiled. "You're going home. We're starting the discharge paperwork now."

I had never heard sweeter words in all my years. "Thank you."

"Don't thank me. Your body did all the work healing up. You'll have to come back for physical therapy as you heal, but otherwise, you should feel a lot better soon."

Chapter 4

"Don't push yourself too hard," Jill said as she wheeled me out the hospital's front entrance. "I don't want to see you back here with a herniated disk."

"She won't," Tracy promised as she helped me to my feet. "I'll make sure of it."

Tracy meant well but I didn't see how she could stop me from exerting myself when she couldn't even make sure she didn't grab me by my broken rib. The pain spiraled through my body and I collapsed onto the ground in front of my mother, who was waiting in the car.

"Becca!" she gasped. She unbuckled her seatbelt and stepped out of the car, rushing over to me.

"Please, nobody touch me," I said. I worked my way to my feet. "I love you all, but you're going to literally kill me with kindness." I looked back at Jill, who must have been debating whether she'd made the best decision, letting me go off with my family. "That's just a turn of phrase."

"Of course," she said. "I hear it all the time. Have a good day, Rebecca. I'll see you in a few days for physical therapy."

"I don't look forward to it," I called after her as she disappeared through the sliding glass doors of the hospital.

"That's not very nice," Mom said. She held out her arms next to me as we walked.

"That's just how we talk to each other," I said.

"Well, I don't like it. I certainly never taught you to talk like that." Mom spun her head toward Tracy. "Did you teach her to talk like that?"

Tracy shook her head. "No, ma'am. I would…never…talk like that."

"Mom." I was hoping to get her off of her tirade. "Can you please open the door for me?"

Mom lurched forward without another word and opened the back door for me. I slid myself into the car, grunting mightily as the seat belt pushed against my broken chest. Tracy knocked on my window, and I gingerly pressed down on the button to lower the glass.

"I'll see you in class tomorrow, yeah?" she asked.

"I don't see how I can avoid it," I replied.

"Please, like you want to avoid it, nerd. I would ask you to pick me up tomorrow, but I guess…I'll see you on the bus?"

"I very much doubt she will be driving much in the near future," my mom said as she slid herself into the front seat. "She won't be driving until she leaves for college."

"Mom!" I said.

"What? I'm not the one who swerved to miss a deer."

"What did you want me to do? Hit it?"

"I wanted you to not fall off a cliff, which you did."

I couldn't argue with her there. I mean, I could since it wasn't the truth, but then I risked unraveling the web of lies I told to prevent anyone from learning about what really happened to me.

"Can we go, please?" I asked.

"Sure thing," Dad said from the driver's seat. "Chauffeur Dad, on the case."

"Be careful, Bob," Mom said. "Don't go too fast over any bumps."

Dad chuckled. "Tell that to the city. These roads are more potholes than asphalt anymore, you know what I mean, kiddo?"

I nodded slowly. "I know what you mean, Dad."

"Just drive, okay?" Mom said. "I'm sure the last thing Becca wants is to sit in the hospital parking lot for any longer than is absolutely necessary."

Dad put the car into gear and made his way out of the hospital. He was careful, but he wasn't wrong about the potholes. The roads in Hillsborough were not very well paved, especially in winter time. It felt like every other rotation of the tires was met by another bump in the road, and every bump put me in such blinding pain than I could barely think.

Part of me didn't mind the pain, though. It distracted me from the dark thoughts swirling in my brain and kept me from dwelling on the flaming eye that called to me from the darkness.

"Are you going to have any trouble getting up the stairs?" Mom asked as Dad pulled into the driveway. The front of our house sat upon a steep hill, and it was a brutal climb to get up to the front door. Our mailman didn't even try any more. He just left the mail on the ledge between the porch railings.

"I'll be fine," I said, carefully exiting the car. I tried my best to play it cool, but my body hurt and ached, and it showed on my face.

Dad was watching me slowly round the back of the car. "We can set up the couch downstairs if you want, pumpkin."

"No, I want my own bed. I've been out of my house long enough. I just want things to get back to normal."

Mom smiled. "That's what we want, too. Normal is good."

"Let me know if you figure out what normal is," Dad added with sad smile.

Things hadn't been normal in a year, not since my sister Mary died. Her death hung over our heads every single day. Mary was the glue that held the family together, and without her I feared we were unraveling. Mom wasn't a caregiver and lacked the maternal instinct my sister had in abundance. It would have been nice for Mom to dote on me like my sister once did, but that wasn't her way. Mary was one in a trillion. Star athlete, Harvard scholar, Dean's list…she was everything that anybody wanted to be, and more.

Except now she was gone.

I pushed open the lime green front door. The smell of lilacs rushed through the air and filled my nostrils. Mom loved flowers. Every season came with new bouquets that filled every room of the house.

After Mary died, Mom filled the house with lilies, even though it was the dead of winter. She called every flower shop in a hundred miles to track them down. Some days, she would be on the phone for over an hour trying to find one arrangement. It was an obsession.

I don't know why I expected the house to change since I'd been gone, but it hadn't. It looked the same as it always did, except that when I left the smell of jasmine filled the house instead of lilac.

Oak lined every floor and piece of furniture and made it feel like we lived in a hunting lodge. Even the couch was trimmed with oak. Mom and Dad always joked that they lived in a vacation house all year round. They used to, anyway. They don't joke that much anymore, at least not without forcing a smile. There was too much hurt.

"I'm going upstairs," I said, heading straight toward the stairs. "I need to sleep."

"Are you sure?" Mom said. "I was going to order pizza."

I paused on the stairs. "I'm not really hungry. I need to get ready for tomorrow, you know."

"Oh," Mom said. "I understand. I just thought that—"

Mom wasn't one to take no for an answer, and she had no problem playing on my guilt.

"All right, Mom," I replied. "Let me go change, and you order the pizza. I have been dying for a hot shower for months. I must smell like a wet cat."

"No," Dad said, walking past me. "You smell worse. Much worse."

Chapter 5

Was there anything more divine than a warm shower?

I certainly didn't think so, especially after not having a real one for over a month. The showers in the hospital were lukewarm at best, and the hospital room was always ice cold, which made getting out of the shower without turning into an icicle a huge challenge. Having a nice, long, steamy shower in a cozy house was the first thing that made me feel like a normal human in weeks.

"Are you doing all right up there?" Mom asked. "You've been in there for a while."

At least thirty minutes, I thought to myself, but I needed it. My hair was ratty and filthy. I hadn't properly washed it since I'd been in the hospital. It wasn't simply my love of long showers which kept me in the bathroom for ages. Most of it was just simple logistics.

Like everything else in my life, taking a shower was something that I'd taken for granted before my accident. It wasn't something I could do easily with a broken arm, torn shoulder ligament, and three busted ribs. Every time I moved my arm, I lost my breath from the excruciating pain of my ribcage and nearly toppled over. Even getting into the shower was a chore, let alone moving my hands to wash myself. Or I should say "hand," since I could only use my left hand to lather and rinse myself. The cast around my right arm needed to be covered with a plastic bag so it wouldn't get wet.

"I'll be right down!" I shouted back, placing my head into the water stream and washing the soap from my eyes.

After letting the water trickle down my back for another minute, I turned off the shower and began the arduous task of drying off. I shook as much water out of my head as I could without passing out from the pain and tied my hair back with a towel. I tied another towel around my chest and wiped the steam off the mirror.

"You really did it to yourself this time, didn't you?" I said to my reflection.

I had never liked my face, but it didn't deserve what I did to it. My nose was no longer splinted, but dark circles still radiated out from it across my face. I didn't like that my nose was long and pointy, but I preferred it to the bulbous, fat eyesore that stared back at me.

I gingerly pulled the plastic bag off my arm and looked down at my cast. Only Tracy had come to see me in the hospital, and she drew a big Pearl from *Steven Universe* shouting, "Get Well Soon" on my cast. At least, that's what she told me it was anyway. She wasn't much of an artist, except on the basketball court.

I stepped out of the bathroom and onto the hardwood floors which lined the hallway. The oak was chilly, so I stepped gingerly on the balls of my feet. My bedroom was right across the way. I took a step towards it, but my body refused to enter. Instead, it pulled me left toward my sister's room at the end of the hallway.

Pictures lined either side of the hall leading to the stairwell across from my sister's room. Her room was in a way better position than mine. She didn't have bathroom smells wafting into her room, and she could sneak out of the house without passing my parent's room.

Across from my parent's room hung big school portraits of my sister and me through the years. She was always smiling perfectly, her bright blue eyes shining out like sapphires while my dull brown ones faded into the background. Her perfect smile lit up the whole house; I just got my braces off last year and I wasn't sure they helped improve my smile very much.

The doorbell rang and Mom scampered across the house to answer it. "Pizza's here!" she shouted after a mumbled exchange with the delivery person.

"Be right down," I called out. "Can't wait."

I lied. I had no interest in food, or the looks my parents gave me which had vacillated between concerned and judgmental since I came out of my coma. However, I needed to eat, if for no other reason than to appease them and keep my own sanity. Soon Mom would come up the stairs and force me to eat at the table, but until then I was perfectly happy meandering through my memories.

I didn't like anything about my sister's room except for its location. If there was such a thing as a stereotypical girl, she was it. Her room was covered in pink hearts, pictures of cute boys adorned her pink walls, and her vanity was home to dozens of different lipstick colors. Mine only had one, black. To be honest, I didn't even want that one shade. It was part of a Halloween costume from years ago and I hadn't bothered throwing it out.

"Not everybody can be as flawless as you," my sister would say to me when I teased her about her drawers full of makeup.

Perfect like her. If she could only see me now. Of course, I guess that's the point. She can't. I was barely holding it together since she left us. Every day was a struggle to stay positive. I used to draw strength from her, and her strength seemed limitless, but now, I didn't know where I'd find it.

"You're not supposed to be in here," Mom said behind me. "What are you doing?"

I had learned how to lie pretty well in the past year. I needed to tell people I was fine when I wasn't, and that they shouldn't worry when they probably should. I learned how to put on a brave face and smile in the face of even my worst days.

"I was trying to find some foundation. For my face. I don't have any and I didn't want people to see me like this." I drew a big circle around my face with my finger. "It might scare people."

Mom gave a forced smile and shook her head. "You'll be fine. Everybody loves you, after all."

"You love me, Mom. That makes you a little bit biased."

She stepped back and gestured down the stairs. "Come down and eat before the pizza gets cold. Your father's stomach is grumbling so loudly that I can hear it all the way up here."

I noticed, of course, Mom didn't say she loved me. She said everybody loved me, and when I tried to probe deeper, she changed the subject. She had been doing that since I was born. Not my sister though, Mom had told Mary that she loved her all the time.

"Coming, Mom," I said with a lying smile.

Chapter 6

"Are you excited about school?" Dad asked after taking way too big a bite of pizza.

"No," I said. Dad's face sagged at my response, so I swallowed my pride and added, "I mean, of course I am, in a way…but I'm also not, in a more tangible way. I haven't seen any of these people in over a month, and none of them have seen me like this. I mean, look at me."

"I think you look great, kiddo," he said. "Don't you think she looks great, Margaret?"

Mom snapped to attention. "Who wants some more garlic bread?"

The woman manipulated and obfuscated, but she did not lie. I liked that about her. She made me feel horrible on a near constant basis, but at least I could count on her to be honest. Dad always lied to make people feel better, which was a good skill to have in certain moments, but when I needed the truth, I asked Mom. When she deflected, you knew your answer.

"It's okay, Dad. I know I look like Hell worn over."

"Rebecca Jean!" Mom's voice boomed. "Language. Just because you are broken and wounded is no reason for bad manners, is it?"

I shook my head. "No, Mom. It isn't. Sorry."

"And straighten your shoulders," she said, pointing to my hunched back. "You look like an orangutan."

"If I do that," I said, "I will be in so much pain I might go back into a coma. Is that what you want?"

"Of course not," she said, looking at me wearily. "Isn't there some middle ground?"

There was never a middle ground with her. The fact she even suggested it was a magnanimous gesture. For her, there was the proper way to do something, and the wrong way.

"I'll try," I said, pulling my shoulders back as far as I could without the pain causing me to vomit. "Better?"

"Well, anything is better than how it was. Now, eat," she said. I thought maybe I could get one day of peace from her relentless badgering when I got home, but I suppose that was too much to ask.

The pizza was a far cry better than the bland, tasteless food from the hospital. Sausage and mushroom were my mother and sister's favorite toppings. I wasn't a fan of either, but I couldn't deny that it tasted wonderful that night, grease and all, as my first meal since leaving the hospital.

"Good, right?" Mom said. "I know it's your favorite."

I chuckled. "Not my favorite, Mom."

"Of course it is. You always loved it—"

"It was Mary's favorite, Mom. I like pepperoni."

"Oh," Mom said. "Well, that's a rather pedestrian choice, don't you think?"

I nodded. "Yes. Probably why I like it."

"Oh dear," she said. "You can be so much better than pedestrian. Though, I suppose you will be a pedestrian for the decided future."

"Ha!" Dad said. "That was funny. Kiddo, did you know your mother was so funny?"

I smirked. "She has her moments. May I be excused?"

"You just started," Mom said. "You must be hungry after all that hospital food."

I placed two more pieces of pizza on my paper plate and stood up. "I have a lot of homework to do still. I don't know if I'll ever catch up."

"Okay, then. I suppose school is more important than anything, isn't it?"

"That's right, Mom. So, I better get to it."

I finished the rest of my pizza in bed after changing into pajamas. I had an essay on Milton's *Paradise Lost* due for English and it was putting me to sleep. I usually enjoyed tales of demons and angels, but Milton had a way with words that could knock me out even if I just drank three pots of coffee.

I placed the book next to my bed and laid back. I had gotten very good sleeping on my back while in the hospital. It helped that any time I moved, there were shooting pains in my ribs. It was good incentive to stay still. My eyes closed, and I fell into sleep.

In the darkness, the haunting image of the flaming eye crowded my vision. A low guttural voice echoed in the darkness.

"I am waiting for you," it said. "I will find you."

"I'm waiting," I replied. "Why can't you find me?"

"We will be together soon."

My eyes sprung open. The eye was just a figment of my imagination, but it felt so real, so very real, as if I could reach out and touch it, and in my heart, I desperately wanted to reach out and touch it. Even as I laid awake, I still wanted to touch it, and be with it forever, and that scared me to no end.

Chapter 7

I didn't sleep for the rest of the night. I couldn't even toss or turn because every move I made was agony. Really, I just stared up at the ceiling all night, with every light on in my room.

Eventually night turned to day, and I slowly rolled out of bed, bleary eyed and exhausted, to prepare for school. I was tired but excited all the same. I really did like school. Most teenagers complained about it, but I knew that the other option was working for a living, and I wasn't ready to do that. School was fine by me.

The bus stop was at the far end of our block, and the cold, winter air nipped against my bones as I walked toward it. No matter which way you walked, the wind on our street always seemed to whip into your face. It was a meteorological phenomenon that I once wrote to our local weatherman about, but I got no response.

I hadn't ridden the bus much since I started high school. My sister drove me to school my freshman and sophomore years. She never complained about it, not even one time. I got my driver's license the winter of tenth grade and bought a car that summer after Mary left for college.

It wasn't much of a car. I loved it though, even though it barely drove. Still, even a piece of garbage puts you ahead of most of the kids who didn't have a car, like Tracy. She relied on me picking her up every morning, which meant she'd been riding the yellow cheese wagon for nearly two months while I recovered in the hospital.

"Jesus Christ. What happened to you?" a squirrelly kid asked. His red hat was too big for his face. Marvin. The only other kid that lived on our street. There used to be a lot of us, but the others all drifted off to college or moved away. I wasn't surprised that he didn't know about what happened to me. He wasn't very popular at school, and nobody on the block talked to his father after his mother walked out on him.

"Nothing." I tried to sound polite.

"Well, that *nothing* messed you up. You look horrible."

He was making me angry. "That's not very nice."

"It's not supposed to be nice," Marvin said. "It's just supposed to be the truth. I don't want you thinking you look all right, and then be embarrassed when people gawk at you."

"Not everybody is as rude as you, Marv."

"Sure they are." Marvin shrugged. "They just don't like to admit it but mark my words they're all gonna judge. Now seriously, what happened to you?"

"I got hit by a bus, Marvin," I said. "Want to see what it feels like?"

I felt bad for Marvin with his broken home and all, but that didn't give him any reason to be a jerk to me, or anybody else.

"Man," Marvin replied. "You Roses have all the luck, don't you? First, your sister dies, and then you get beaten up by a sasquatch."

I could have used my sister's death as my own excuse to be a jerk, but Mary would have been so disappointed if I let that happen. She pitied Marvin, and was always nice to him, even when nobody else was. That didn't mean I had to take Marvin's verbal abuse, though.

"Watch it, kid," I growled. "You're cruisin'."

"I'd like to see you try," Marvin replied.

Marvin talked a big game but had a glass jaw. He was just another kid who acted like hot stuff to mask the fact he was a loser.

"You can keep putting me on, but I really want to know," Marvin said. "What happened to you?"

I sighed. "You know the road around Gordon's Gorge?"

"Yeah, I know it. Scares the piss out of me every time we drive up it. I always think we're going to fall off."

"With good reason, it turns out."

"Wait," he said, standing up straight. "You got that driving off the gorge?"

"Afraid so," I said, wincing. The crisp air pained my lungs, which caused everything else to throb and ache.

"Wow, I guess you're lucky, then."

"I wouldn't call myself lucky, Marvin."

"Well, you're not dead, are ya?" he replied. "I figure if you fell off that gorge you should be dead for sure. Makes me feel a little better, honestly."

"Yeah, well…" I frowned.

Mercifully, the yellow school bus turned the corner before Marvin could ask me any more questions. He pushed past me and onto the bus first, and I followed gingerly behind. The driver smiled as bright as she could, even if it was pretty clear she hated being a bus driver.

Tracy beckoned me to come to the back seat toward her, but I just couldn't wander that far back. I hadn't even gotten to school and I was already exhausted from the pain in my chest. The bus lurched forward, and I gasped. It was going to be a long day.

Chapter 8

Tracy ran up to me after we got off the bus and grabbed the backpack out of my hand. "You shouldn't be carrying that."

"Maybe not," I replied. "Not much of a choice, though. It's not like I have a valet."

"I'll be your valet," she said. "How much does it pay?"

"Nothing."

"Nothing?" she replied. "Not even in cookies?"

"Not even in cookies."

She thought for a moment, then passed the backpack to me. "Forget that. Not interested. Frankly, I don't know who you're going to find to help you for slave wages."

I grabbed the book bag from her and grunted as I slung it onto my back. "I suppose I'll just have to do it myself, then."

"Yeah, you will," she replied, before her face turned down. "Are you nervous?"

"I've been going to this school for two and a half years," I said, walking with the sea of kids heading for the front entrance. "I think I have the hang of it."

"Yeah, but now everybody's looking at you as the broken girl."

"Are they?" I said. "Am I broken?"

"Well, yeah." Tracy gestured toward my broken face, arm, and chest. "I mean, look at you."

"I didn't think it was that noticeable."

It was easy to play it off in my head that nobody would care about my new look, but it was a much different thing when hundreds of eyes turned to me when I walked past them. I tried not to care that they were looking at me, but I still wished they would stare somewhere else. I wasn't some circus freak.

"Oh my god," I said. "People have to deal with this all the time, don't they?"

"High school's cruel, Bec," Tracy replied, holding the door open for me. "For some people it's crueler than others."

"Well, it's not going to be cruel to me. I'm not going to let it."

"As if you have a choice," Tracy said, shaking her head. "Hey, have you talked to the coach yet?"

I shook my head. "No. I was heading there now. Why?"

"Oh, no reason. Just remember I'm a good friend, okay?"

There was just enough time before class to meet with Coach Glazer in her office next to the gym. If Tracy didn't stop talking, I'd miss my chance to catch up with Glazer and let her know I was back in school.

"I don't—"

"Just promise me, okay?"

I rolled my eyes, exasperated. "Okay, fine."

"Good," Tracy said, turning on her heels to walk away. "Bye then. Gotta go."

"You are so weird!" I shouted after her.

Dunwich High School made a big deal out of our successful teams. We were winners, having won the regional title seven times in the past decade, and state once. I intended to take us back to state when I became captain next year, if my body healed properly.

"Coach?" I said, walking into Coach Glazer's office. Gameplay schematics were strewn everywhere, and she was staring at her playbook.

"Rebecca Rose!" Coach Glazer said. She jumped up and held out her right hand. "As I live and breathe."

I pointed to my right arm, still in a cast. "Sorry, but I can't…do…that."

Coach Glazer pulled her hand away. "Of course. Sorry. Force of habit."

"It's okay."

Coach slid back around her desk and sat down. The pungent smell of rancid sweat permeated the small office. She kept additional equipment and uniforms in her office and apparently, she didn't make a habit of cleaning them properly before storage.

"What can I help you with, Rose? Here to reclaim your spot on the team? Sorry, but I just can't—"

"Reclaim?" I said. "You gave away my spot?"

Coach looked up, squinting. "Didn't Tracy tell you?"

"No. Tracy did not tell me."

"Oh," Coach said. "I guess that's to be expected. I'm sure she didn't want to upset you."

"I'm off the team?" I exclaimed. "Just like that?"

"I mean, not just like that. These are…extenuating circumstances."

"That's not fair!" I shouted.

"Listen, kid," Coach Glazer said. "It's a tough break but look at you. You aren't any good to anyone out there. We have to field a squad that can take us to state, and you're just not it right now. I look forward to having you back next year, though."

"Next year?" I said. "I'm almost out of this cast. I can still make it back by the end of the season."

"And then what?" Coach Glazer said. "You'll be at half strength at best. You'll need at least a year to get back into physical shape. There will be a spot for you next year, though. I know you'll work hard at it."

"Isn't there anything I can do to change your mind?"

She shook her head. "It sure is a shame, though. You were a great talent."

"I *am* a great talent," I replied. "And I'll be back next year. You just wait and see."

"I hope so, kid. I really do."

I wanted to pop out of my cast and strangle Coach Glazer, but that wouldn't have helped matters. So instead of a fight, I simply turned and walked out, working hard to bottle up my anger. I took a step into the hallway and smacked into a girl walking at full speed. The impact knocked me over and sent me flying to the ground. Pain seared up my arm into my shoulder and I cried out.

"Hey!" I heard a voice from above me. "Are you okay?"

I blinked, my eyes watering. "Do I look okay?"

The girl wore dark eyeliner thick enough to be bags under her eyes. Her skin was pasty white. Thin locks of green hair poked out from a black hoodie embossed with a skeleton down the front of it.

"Let me help you up," she said, holding out her hand.

"I don't need your help, or your pity." I tried pushing myself up off the ground with one hand but lost my balance and slammed onto the ground again.

"I don't pity you, dude," she said. "I just feel bad about knocking you over."

She held out her arm again, and I took it. "Feeling bad…that's pity."

"No, it's not. Dude, why are you so mad at me? It was an accident."

"You pushed me over." I rubbed my shoulder. "It hurt."

"Yeah, and I apologized, and helped you up. You know what, whatever, I don't care."

"I'm not surprised. Why would you care?"

The girl pulled off her hood and pulled her silky, green hair back into a ponytail. Her sleeves rode up and exposed her wrists, showing the jagged horizontal scars cut there, bulging pink on her otherwise flawless skin.

"Exactly," she said. "I don't. You have to care about somebody to pity them. Just watch where you're going next time, all right?"

She didn't wait for me to respond. She just brushed past me on her way down the hallway. I had only been in school for a couple minutes, and I had already been knocked over twice. Once literally. This was not a good omen for the day to come.

Chapter 9

My first day back at school sucked exponentially more than I thought possible. It was hard for me to remember having a horrible day at school before. There were times I didn't want to go because I was tired or sick, and I'd definitely been severely bored in class on more than one occasion, but I hadn't ever had a truly horrible day at school until that day.

In first period, my English teacher called my views on Milton's tedious work trite and uninteresting…It's Milton that's trite and uninteresting, and I'll never be convinced otherwise. On top of that, she gave me four additional essays that Tracy forgot to give me while I was in the hospital.

My math teacher showed me the long string of zeros next to my name and I swear I just about fainted on the spot. Even though I handed in ten assignments to him, they barely made a dent in what I had missed while I was in the hospital.

To top it off, I had to take all my notes with my left hand, and I am not left handed, so I could barely read what I wrote. After school, I didn't have anything to do since I'd been kicked off the basketball team and all. I had to take the bus home like a normal sucker. Tracy wasn't even with me since she was at practice.

The only person who kept me company was Marvin, and…no, thank you. I was used to getting home and having the bustling house ready with dinner. However, when I got home after school that first day, the only thing that welcomed me home was empty silence.

I didn't like that sort of quiet. It was where the flaming eye lived, calling out to me. I thought maybe I could drown out the emptiness with television, but not even *Steven Universe* could make me feel better. After a few hours of television, I resigned myself to a lifetime of homework upstairs. Luckily, with my persistent nightmares, I never felt like sleeping again, so I gained eight additional hours every day to catch up on my mountain of homework.

I trudged up the stairs, but I couldn't make it past Mary's room before the emptiness came back upon me like it had never left. I dropped my book bag and took a deep breath, then another, trying to let the feeling pass, but it wouldn't leave me. The world was cold and lonely, and no matter what I did I couldn't shake the feeling that life would be better if I wasn't in it.

"I really need to talk to you, Mary," I said to the empty room, and to the reflection of myself in the vanity mirror. "I wish you were still here."

I walked inside her room and took a seat on her bed. I didn't know what was going on with me, but I knew that Mary would understand. She was the most positive person in the world, maybe that the world had ever known. Yet there had to be a darkness inside her as well.

There had to be, for her to do what she did. After all, she killed herself. I didn't like to say those words, but it was true. I avoided the word "suicide" as much as possible, but that didn't change the cold hard, truth of the matter.

We didn't ever talk about it, but I knew Mom and Dad thought about Mary's death in their dark moments, when they were by themselves. They thought about it in the quiet times, just like I did. They thought about how their perfect daughter could take a bottle of pills and kill herself.

Not Mary.

Mary was perfect. Mary was better than me in me in every way. We never thought she would...

I was there when Mom got the call, so I knew it was true. I was there when we drove up to the college. I was there, waiting outside the morgue, when Mom identified the body. I was there. I saw Mary, so I knew it was true, but I didn't believe it. Most days, I still don't believe it. I figure she ran away, or she had a really bad fight with Mom. One day, she will be home again. She has to be.

"Why?" I said as I crumpled over on her bed.

Mom hadn't moved anything since my sister left for school. Everything remained in perfect order. Only one thing was added to my sister's room since she died. In her school belongings was a spiral bound notebook that she wrote in every day. My mother hadn't opened it and forbade me from doing so as well. I wanted so badly to read what was inside, but I respected my mother's wishes.

Mary was the most perfect person I ever knew. I wanted to grow up to be like her. She was captain of field hockey, president of the student body, and valedictorian. Everybody loved her, and everything worked out for her. I modeled myself after her. I was first in my class before the accident and headed to be captain of the basketball team next year, but even that wasn't enough to be as great as Mary. But she had taken her own life. What did that mean for me? Was I doomed to follow in my sister's footsteps?

My body seized in pain as I sobbed uncontrollably on my sister's bed. I cried until I had nothing left inside me, then fell asleep. Something about her bed must have been magical, because I did not dream of the flaming eye when I slept there. Instead, I dreamt of unicorns.

Chapter 10

"Are you excited to get your cast off today?" Mom asked. We were on the way to the doctor's office.

"Sure."

The truth was, I wasn't excited for much recently. School had been a bear for the past week, and every waking minute was filled with stiffness and pain. Whenever I slept in my own bed, I dreamt of the darkness or, worse, the flaming eye that beckoned me to join it.

The only respite I got from its haunting voice was sleeping in my sister's bed. That meant sneaking out of my room every night and crawling into her bed, sure to get up before my mother did the next morning.

"It must be nice to think about life getting back to normal, right?" Mom said.

Normal. I wasn't even sure what that meant any more. I'm not sure I ever knew what it meant, frankly. I liked to believe that my life was normal before, when I had straight-A's and a star status on the basketball court. Whatever it was, normal or not, I missed it.

I missed being the smartest girl in class. It had been a massive struggle to catch up ever since I returned to school. I managed to complete half my missed assignments while I was in the hospital, but new work just kept piling up on top of the old. I couldn't get caught up, and I didn't understand any of the material.

"What's normal?" I asked.

"Well, not having casts on for one thing," Mom replied.

"Lots of people have casts, or their legs don't work, or some other sort of thing is wrong with them. Does that mean they're not normal?"

"Kind of?" my mother said, even though her reply sounded more like a question than anything else. "I mean, if you want to get technical about it—"

"I think you can just stop now, Mom, before you dig your hole any deeper."

"Oh, thank God," she said. "Which reminds me, once you get home after school tonight, we need to go to church. I have the Father saying mass in our name. Well, in your name, at least."

"I don't really feel like church, Mom."

"Nobody really feels like church, dear. It's just a thing you do."

"I have homework."

"It can wait."

"You wouldn't say that if you knew how much of it I had, or how far behind I am in my coursework."

"I'm sure it will all work out. Now, please don't embarrass me. It's an insult if you're not there when they dedicate a mass to you."

"They dedicate masses to dead people all the time and the dead never show up. Is that an insult, too?"

"No, but this is different."

"How?"

Mom thought for a second. "Look, you know I don't like playing the 'Mom' card, but I'm afraid you're just going to have to do it because I said so."

I chuckled. "Mom, I mean this with all the respect it deserves, but you love playing the Mom card."

"Either way, you have to come."

"Whatever." I slouched lower in my seat.

We drove the rest of the way in blissful silence, though the tension between us sank deeper. I was grateful to get out of the car and into the doctor's office. "Hi," I said, walking up to the thin, dark-skinned woman working the front desk. "I have—"

"We have a four o'clock with the doctor," my mother butted in. As if "we" had anything.

"Yes, we need to remove *our* cast from *our* arm," I growled.

It was twenty minutes before the receptionist led us into an exam room, and another thirty before Doctor Montrell joined us, but it was worth the wait.

"Thank god," I said, slowly bending my right arm. It was the greatest feeling in my life, being able to move again. I had full range of motion.

"Don't go too fast, all right?" the doctor said. "I know it feels like you're back to normal, but your muscles haven't had to work in a long time, so just go slow, and make sure not to miss your physical therapy appointments."

"I haven't missed one yet," I said. I was still going once a week, even though I felt perfectly healthy and recovered. "Do you think I can play basketball soon?"

Doctor Montrell shrugged. "It's possible. The question is, can you play it well?"

"I can play amazing, but am I going to hurt myself if I try?"

"Give it a little time, okay? You're still healing."

"Time is not something I have."

Doctor Montrell gave a chuckle. "That's what I thought too, when I was your age. When you get to be my age though, you start to realize you had nothing but time as a teenager, and you'll miss it."

"Boy howdy, isn't that the truth," my mother chimed in from the chair in the corner of the room. She hadn't said much since the doctor came in. She just scowled out the window, watching the cars flow in and out of the parking lot.

"It doesn't feel like that to me," I said.

"And it won't for a long time," Doctor Montrell smiled. "If you don't take your time, though, you're going to regret it."

"For how long?" I said. "Will I regret it, I mean."

"For the rest of your life, which let me assure you, is a very long time."

Chapter 11

I'd wanted to be seen as a good girl ever since I was a child, and good girls went to church. At least, that's what my mother said. I still went when Mary stopped going, and when she…when she…

I went even more after that.

I attended church dutifully every week. Sometimes, I sang in the choir and when I was younger, I even attended youth retreats. I was baptized, confirmed, and kept up holy days of obligation, which, like, nobody does.

Still, I won't tell you that I particularly enjoyed church. I won't say that I got much out of it, because that would be a lie. I enjoyed the community, that was true, and every once in a while, the priest said something that resonated with me, but for the vast majority of weeks, I counted down the minutes until it was time to go. I was just lucky that we were Roman Catholic, so the priest kept it a tight forty-five.

My sister loved church when she was my age. She swayed back and forth during the hymns and seemed genuinely moved. Of course, that was before she went off to school. After that, she stopped going completely.

Part of me believed that if she'd had a better church community at college maybe she wouldn't have…done what she ended up doing, but it was hard to blame anyone for that, except my sister. Even then, it was hard to blame her. I read all about depression and anxiety after she killed herself, and I knew it was a disease, but I just can't help being bitter at her for leaving me, for leaving us.

The priest of our church was Father Bennett, a kindly, old man who nobody ever accused of molesting children. It was a terrible thing to say, but I'm always suspicious of any priest who had been in the clergy for more than thirty years. Many had suspicious proclivities, so it was important to note ours was not known to be a pedophile. I'm sure most priests were not pedophiles, but that's not what the news would have you believe.

Father Bennett's sermons were short, which I liked, but boring, which I didn't. His voice was dull and monotonous, without any of the rich complexity of my friends' more evangelical sermons at their church. But he was brief, and for that I was eternally thankful. In a world that never stopped, who had time for a two-hour lecture on morality?

Tracy did, I guess, since she went to the Baptist church on the other side of town. I went with her several times. Her church was lively, which I liked, but lasted forever, which I didn't. You had to pick your battles in this world, and I had chosen mine. I wanted the shortest service possible, even if it was boring as sin.

"Hello, Father," Mom said, walking out of the church after a particularly brief mass. "Good to see you again."

"Good evening," Father Bennett said. "So nice of you to come. I hope you enjoyed the service."

"Thank you so much for dedicating this mass to my dear daughter," Mom said before I could respond.

The priest smiled. "Happy to do it. Nice to see Rebecca is still with us. Did you enjoy the mass, my dear?"

Father Bennett's evening sermons are even shorter than his Sunday ones. When Mom took me to church that night, he only talked for ten minutes before he started wrapping it up. I wish I could remember what he talked about, but then again, I just didn't care enough to pay close attention.

"It was lovely and brief," I replied. "My two favorite things. A very fitting mass to be dedicated in my honor. I'm very thankful."

"Yes. Well, people are tired after work," Father said, smacking his lips. "No need to drag it on, don't you agree?"

"I do. And I appreciate it greatly."

We shook hands, and his hand lingered on mine for a moment. "I remember your baptism. Do you know that?"

"I didn't."

"It was a lovely affair. You wore a yellow dress and cried when I placed the holy water on your forehead."

"I'm sure my crying had nothing to do with you."

"No," he replied, eyes looking off into space. "It rarely does. Sometimes they cry, sometimes they don't. You never can tell. Your sister, she didn't cry. She was a perfect baby."

"That tracks," I replied with a sigh.

At my sister's funeral he talked about the beauty of a short life and honoring every moment we had on this earth. My sister would have loved it. She would have cried. Even I shed a tear, but less for the sermon and more for the loss of my sister.

"Well," I said. "We should be going."

"Yes," my mother added. "It was a lovely service, Father. Thank you again."

"See?" Mom said as we walked away. "Don't you feel better coming?"

I wanted to tell her no. I wanted to say it was a waste of me time, but that was a fight I didn't need to have. So instead, I just smiled and nodded.

"I do, Mom. Thanks."

There was no need for a fight. After all, the service was brief, which I did appreciate, and it filled the silence, which I appreciated even more.

Chapter 12

I didn't particularly like physical therapy. I enjoyed exercise, but Jill took it easy on me. I could push myself further and harder than Jill wanted me to, but every time I tried to take it to the next level, she tugged me back.

"Don't pull too hard!" Jill said as I yanked the resistance bands harder than I ever had before. "Stop!"

"I can do more!" I said with a wince, pulling the resistance band back to my shoulder.

"And I'm telling you to stop," Jill said with a stern voice.

I met Jill at her physical therapy studio so I could get the work in without having to return to the hospital, a place I hated. The hospital didn't do anything to make me hate it. If anything, it had saved my life, but it was also the place where I'd been the weakest I'd ever been. I had no interest in returning any time soon.

"Sorry," I said, releasing the band. "I'm just excited."

"Well, you're twice as ambulatory as you were before, so I'm not surprised, but you're not full strength yet."

"I know," I panted. "How much longer?"

"Until what?"

"Until I'm full strength."

"I'm sure that your doctor told you, but you need to take your time. There is no perfect timetable."

I nodded. "I know, I know, and I know you all think I'm young, and I've got plenty of time, but I'm the one who has to live in this body, all right? I'm sick of things taking longer, and people pitying me, and Mom having to drive me around. I'm not an invalid, all right?"

Jill placed her hand on mine. "I know you're not, but I'm trying to prevent you from doing permanent damage. I know you think you're young and invincible now, but one day you'll be old, and broken, like me. You don't want to do something you'll regret for the rest of your life."

I sighed. "It's hard."

"I know. Waiting is the hardest part, as Tom Petty would say, and he's a wise man. Before long, you'll be shooting hoops with the best of them, but until then, just take it easy, okay? Don't red-line yourself just to prove you're normal."

I wiped my forehead with my forearm. "Fine."

The door behind Jill swung open. The goth girl who bumped into me a couple of weeks ago walked through the door and sat down in the waiting area.

"Do you know that girl?" I said, pointing to her.

"She's my next appointment. Why?"

"She goes to my school."

The girl was wearing the same scowl and skeleton hoodie that she had when she bowled me over in front of Coach Glazer's office. I felt bad about how I treated her. It wasn't her fault she was clumsy, and that I hadn't been paying attention.

"Why is she here?" I asked.

"You know I can't tell you that. Patient-doctor confidentiality."

"But you aren't a doctor."

"HIPAA is a tough mistress. What are you going to do?"

"I'm going to talk to her," I said, pushing myself to my feet.

"That's not—oh whatever. Go for it. We're done here anyway."

I pushed off the floor and grabbed my purse. "Hey," I said, walking up to the girl. "How are you doing? Funny to see you here."

She barely glanced at me. "Don't talk to me."

"Excuse me?" I asked. "I'm just trying—"

"I know what you're trying to do, and I reject it. Just because we're in the same place doesn't mean we're the same. That goes for school, and it goes for here. If you ever see me again," she said, pushing off the seat, "it will go for then, too."

What a jerk, I thought as she brushed past me and smiled at Jill. I realized then that she hated me, and I didn't like that feeling. I don't know why she was so different. Lots of people probably hated me, but I really needed her not to be one of them. Luckily, my best friend knew everything about everybody at Dunwich High. Unluckily, I was mad at her.

Chapter 13

I hadn't talked to Tracy since she failed to warn me about Coach Glazer kicking me off the basketball team. It was the longest fight we've ever had. Previously, the longest fight we ever had was seventeen minutes and began after she told me that Drake was lame, and I proceeded to correct her ridiculous claim.

I guess I shouldn't call this a fight, though. It was really a one-sided irritation. I was pissed at her and she was sorry. The longer it dragged on, and the more I snubbed her, the more angry she got. I think it was because she didn't have anybody to unload all her juicy gossip to, personally, but I'm sure it also had something to do with the fact that I was acting like an immature child.

In my defense, I was being treated like an immature child by almost everybody in my life. I guess some of it rubbed off on me. Now, though, I had a reason to bury the hatchet, because Tracy had information that I desperately wanted. I would need to talk with her.

I couldn't find her during the school day, but I knew she had basketball practice every afternoon. That's where I should have been, too. Walking into the gym without my trainers and gym clothes on made my heart ache.

The team was going through shooting drills, and Tracy was paired with a couple of other guards: Crystal, a senior with a strong perimeter game, and Rita, who must have taken my place on the team. She was on JV last year, and barely missed getting on varsity this season. She wasn't as good as I was on defense but could drive well enough that it wasn't completely insulting that she replaced me. Rita might not be much of an asset, but at least she wasn't a liability.

"Hey," I said, walking up to Tracy as she took foul shots. "Can we talk?"

"I guess," Tracy replied without looking at me. She bounced the ball a few times. "This is a weird way to ignore me."

"About that," I said. "I was thinking about not doing that anymore."

"What do you want then?" Tracy said, taking another shot.

"Why do I have to want something?"

"Cuz, that's what you do. You get mad until you need something, and then you come back."

"Rose!" Coach Glazer shouted from across the gym. "What are you doing here?"

"Sorry, Coach!" I called back. "I just need to talk with Tracy for a second."

"This better be important."

"It is."

"Fine." Coach Glazer fumed. "Tracy, take five, then get back into it. We're not running a slumber party here."

Tracy tossed the ball to Rita and walked with me toward the bench. "You're gonna get me in trouble."

"She'll get over it."

"I don't want her to get over it. I want to not be in trouble in the first place."

"I'm sorry," I replied. "Not just for getting you in trouble, but for everything. I know you were just looking out for me."

"I really was," Tracy said. "Or at least, I thought I was. It was a crappy thing to do, not telling you, and I'm sorry, too."

"Good."

"So," Tracy said. "That was really hard for you. You must need something big."

"I wouldn't call it big…per se."

"I knew you needed something!" Tracy said, grinning ear to ear. "Well, come on. Out with it."

"Do you know a goth girl, green hair, who wears a skeleton hoodie a lot?"

"Yeah," she nodded. "She's in my math class. Total freak show."

"Why does she have scars, on her wrist, like she cut herself?"

Tracy sighed. "Wow, you really are out of the loop, aren't you? That happened like, two years ago."

"I don't even know where the loop is, that's how far out of the loop I am on things. I expect you to tell me these things. You are my loop."

"Well, you didn't know her, so why would I tell you about her? Wait, why do you want to know anyway?"

I paused for a long moment. I didn't want to admit the truth. "She…doesn't like me."

Tracy laughed. "Oh, wow. You really are that shallow. You need to make this girl like you just to what, feel validated?"

I scratched my head. "I don't know. Yes, no. Come on. Can you help me or not?"

Tracy chuckled. "Literally everybody in this school loves you."

I threw up my arms. "Not literally. She doesn't. And I'm not feeling the love at all recently."

"So, you get all stalkery and weird?"

"I'm not weird!" I said. "I just…want her to like me."

Tracy shook her head. "You have problems."

"Don't you think I know that?" I asked, placing my head in my hands. "Can you help me or not?"

Tracy furrowed her brow. "I don't know if I should, but I will, because I love you, and I want you to stop hating me."

"I never hated you."

"Fine, whatever," Tracy said, shaking her head in disbelief. "Do you remember Tommy Bender? He was a senior when we were freshman. He played soccer."

I thought for a moment, but the name only sounded vaguely familiar. "Kind of. Didn't something happen to him?"

Tracy bit her lip. "Yeah, I'll say. He died in a car crash before prom."

I nodded. "That I remember vaguely."

Tracy took a long pause, then sighed deeply. "The freak show you're talking about is Trisha."

I looked at her blankly. "Is that name supposed to mean something to me?"

"Um, yeah," Tracy scoffed. "She was Tommy's girlfriend. She was in the car when he got t-boned by that truck. He died on the spot. She was hurt pretty bad, too. Had to have like a dozen surgeries."

I held my hand on my mouth, shocked. "Oh my god. That's horrible."

"Yeah, and I heard, that after that she went into a dark, deep funk, and that's when…"

I grabbed her arm as she drifted off, lost in thought. "When what?"

Tracy gave me a searching look. "Are you sure it's not going to trigger you? Like, I'm scared you're going to wig out about your sister if I go on and tell you any more information."

"I'll be fine," I said, looking down at the ground. "Seriously, I need to hear this."

"Fine," Tracy replied. "But I warned you."

"Noted."

Tracy waited for a moment, not sure if she should keep going. Then she gathered her nerves and continued, "She went into a really dark place, and that's when she tried to kill herself."

She had tried to kill herself, just like my sister. The only difference was that Trisha failed while my sister succeeded. God, that is morbid. I've never been a fan of morbidity, but now it lived inside of me all the time, and I couldn't shake it.

Tracy placed her hand on my shoulder. "You going to be okay?"

I nodded, staring at the floor. "Yeah, I think so."

"Morris!" Coach shouted to Tracy. "Time's up! Let's go."

Tracy grabbed my hand and pulled me to my feet. "Come on. I know what will cheer you up." Tracy pulled me across the gym toward where Rita and Crystal were still practicing foul shots. "Throw me one of those balls."

Crystal passed a ball to Tracy, who dribbled it deftly toward the line. When we reached the line, she stuffed the ball into my stomach.

"Go for it."

I looked back at the coach. "Isn't she going to be pissed?"

"You're already in her dog house, Bec. At least we can get some use out of it by showing her you can still play."

I looked up at the basket. "I'm not sure if I can. Doc says—"

"It's one basket. Just shoot it already. Don't be a wimp."

I bounced the basketball twice on the ground. It felt good in my hands. I closed my eyes and took a deep breath. I opened them and looked up at the basket. One more bounce and I took my shot. The ball glided off my fingers. I hadn't realized how much I missed the feel of the ball leaving my hand.

I smiled as I watched the ball glide to the basket. I knew I made it before it even went through the net, but I nearly teared up when I heard the swish. I looked back at Coach who just stared at me.

"I'll see you around," I said to Tracy with a smile. I didn't tell her that my shoulder and arm throbbed after just that one shot, but the fact I was able to shoot at all was amazing, given where I was just a couple weeks before.

"When?" Tracy asked.

"Can you come to the mall with me? I need to get a job so I can buy another car."

"Is your Mom gonna let you do that?"

"I don't care."

"Then, sure."

Chapter 14

One of the most embarrassing experiences of my life was trying to grovel for my job back at Taco Bell. Even more embarrassing was the fact that it didn't work. The place sucked, but there weren't a ton of jobs around town, and I desperately needed one.

"What is your mother going to say when you come home with a car?" Tracy said as we walked from school to the mall. It was only a half a mile from the school.

"Let's be fair, I'm making minimum wage at best. It's not like I'm going to be able to afford a car for a long while. Maybe Mom will be dead by then."

"Dark," she said. "When did you get so dark?"

"A while ago."

The Royal Maple Mall was once the highlight of town. It was the biggest outlet mall in the entire country when it was built, which we took a lot of pride in having that badge of honor. In its heyday it had people coming from hundreds of miles to shop for a deal.

Those days were long gone now, though. Mom says the place is a shell of its former self. I never knew the mall to be anything but a kind of scuzzy place that needed a paint job, but that still didn't take away from the fact it was walking distance from school and had a ton of stores. I figured I would be able to find a job there easily.

I figured wrong. We walked every inch of the mall multiple times, and not one place was hiring. Since it was after Christmas, places were more likely to fire their seasonal workers than to hire new ones.

"We've been up and down this mall for three hours, Bec," Tracy said, dragging herself listlessly through the empty corridors of the mall.

"I just want to go a couple more places," I replied.

"Where else could we possibly go that hasn't already told you no?"

My sister used to like hanging out at the mall when she was in high school. She and her friends walked over after practice, spent some money, and caught the last bus back home. I never cared much for hanging out with people when I wasn't doing an activity, except for Tracy, and we could do that anywhere, including at home, in pajamas. Just another way my sister was better than me at something else, socializing with other humans.

"I don't know, Trace. Maybe there's some heretofore unknown section of the mall which could take us to Diagon Alley or something."

"Oh, now that's interesting," Tracy said. "Do you think they hire high school workers in Diagon Alley?"

"I'm not sure. Everybody who worked at the shops seemed like they were old."

"Yeah, but that couldn't be, though, right? Take Olivander. He was always at the wand shop in the books, but he had wand shops all over the world. He can't be everywhere at once, and it's not like he's paying more than minimum wage. That place was filthy. Or George. Do you think he was constantly at the sweets shop? Even for somebody filled with childlike wonder, the scream of little kids must get on his ever-loving nerves. No, the only people who could put up with them are high school kids that had no other options in life."

"Didn't George die?"

"No, George lost an ear."

"Which would mean he couldn't hear so well when people came to the shop."

"And that means he needed help all the time, right? And there are only so many high school witches with big accounts at Gringotts's. The rest had to work for a living."

That was what I loved most about Tracy. When I was feeling terrible, she always tried to cheer me up. Usually it worked too, but this time I couldn't shake the feeling that everything was doomed, and I was useless.

"You've convinced me. I think that they all exploited high school labor."

"Me too," Tracy said with a smile. "What do you think the minimum wage was then? Galleon an hour?"

I sat down on the bench outside of a derelict Levi's outlet. Through the window, I could see two girls folding clothes. Their shoulders were hunched, and they looked all-around hopeless and defeated. Possibly they even wished for death to relieve them from their work. I so wanted to be them.

"Ugh. That seems so low."

"Well, a galleon is about six bucks, according to Wikipedia," Tracy said, looking at her phone. "And the minimum wage here is like seven-fifty, so it's probably like one galleon, a couple sickles, and a few knuts."

I sighed deeply. "What am I gonna do, Trace? I need a car to get away from my Mom. I need a job to get a car, and nobody is hiring."

"It's quite the dilemma," she sighed. "I know what will make you feel better though. How about a smoothie?"

"I don't have money for Jamba Juice," I said. "I don't have money for anything."

"I know." Tracy pulled out her purse. "But I do."

"How do you have money?" I stared at her, my mouth open. "You never have money."

I had known Tracy for most of my life, and I had never seen her have one cent to her name, or at least any that she was willing to spend on me. I must have been a sad sight for her to offer to buy something for me.

"It was just Christmas. Just because you were asleep during it doesn't mean the rest of us didn't make out like bandits. I didn't get you anything, so consider this your gift."

"You know what?" I said, standing up. "I am going to be the mooch for once and let you buy me that Jamba Juice."

"Really?" Tracy said, depressed. "I was kinda hoping you were gonna have too much pride for it."

"New year, new me."

"And this new you is a jobless mooch?"

"That's right."

"And you're okay with that?"

"Indubitably."

Chapter 15

"Hello," Tracy said, walking up to the counter of the Jamba Juice in the mall's food court. "I have a coupon for a two-for-one Jamba Juice."

She reached into her purse and pulled out a coupon. I didn't have to look to know it was expired. Tracy would get her discount anyway, though. I had seen it a thousand times before.

"This coupon is expired," the scraggly-faced cashier said.

"Is it?" Tracy replied. Her voice was a higher pitch than normal. "Oh no. But I only have money for one." She turned to me. "I know it's your birthday, so I'll just let you have it, sis."

I knew better than to question Tracy when she was in character. "No, Gabby. You should have it. You worked so hard for that money."

"I won't hear of it," Tracy said. "Pick anything you want." She was forcing herself to cry and choking back her crocodile tears. "There's always more money."

The cashier leaned forward. "You know what, I'll just give it to you. It's okay."

"Really?" Tracy said, her eyes lighting up. "That would be wonderful."

"Sure," the cashier replied. "This place sucks anyway. Screw them."

Tracy turned to me, a broad smile on her face. She took great satisfaction in bending people to her will. Watching her brimming with pride warmed the cockles of my heart.

Maybe I should have cared about lying more, but my smoothie cheered me right up, so it was hard to care about scamming a faceless corporation out of a few bucks. A cold smoothie in the middle of winter might not sound that appealing, but it was all I had in the world that wasn't trying to judge me—Tracy, and a stupid smoothie. For the ten minutes it took me to finish, I enjoyed the hecking life out of it.

It was true. Everybody seemed to be judging every little thing I did, and I was a little on edge. My teachers judged me when my homework wasn't up to the quality they expected from me. My parents judged me because I wasn't the happy, peppy kid they knew before the accident. Don't even get me started on my friends, who didn't even want to be around me anymore for some reason. If I couldn't do something for them, like help them win basketball games, then what good was I?

I guess everything good comes to an end. Things used to be smooth sailing for me. I chose the word "good" carefully. I wasn't sure bad things ended. Bad things seemed to stack on top of each other, like a horrible game of Jenga, where there are no good places to pull out a brick without it toppling down upon you, forever.

That's how I felt these days, at least. I had thought the foundation of my life was on pretty-solid footing. People marveled at my fortitude when I didn't break down after my sister's death. I kept right on moving forward, like a steam engine barreling toward a tunnel. Mary would have been proud of me for that. She would have done the same thing, taken my death in stride and kept on moving, because that was the kind of person she was. Nothing frazzled her.

I wasn't as strong as she was, as much as I wanted to pretend I measured up. Maybe my sister's death was the moment the tower started to teeter. Maybe somebody took a brick from the bottom of my Jenga set and made it unstable. Maybe every day since then, people have taken my blocks, little by little, until there was nothing left but a holey, old, Swiss cheese tower, so wobbly that a light breeze could knock it over.

"Are you okay?" Tracy asked. She was sipping the last of her smoothie.

"Of course," I said, though she had startled me, I was so deep in thought. "Why?"

"You haven't said anything in like, five minutes. I've had nothing but the horrible mall music to keep me company."

"Sorry. I didn't even know. I zoned out."

"Duh," Tracy said, leaning forward. "That's why I asked if everything was okay with you?"

I shook my head. "No, Trace. Nothing is all right. I'm just trying to do the best I can."

She sighed. "Oh. Yeah. Well, I get that."

"You get that?" I said. "You're the happiest person I know."

"That doesn't mean I don't deal with dark stuff, you know? You don't have a monopoly on brooding. I just do it in private, like a normal person."

"What makes that normal?"

"The fact that people say it's normal. The fact that it doesn't bum everybody else out. The fact that I don't alienate my friends for weeks for no reason."

"Hey now. I had a reason."

Tracy took another sip. "The fact that I didn't drive off a cliff and worry everybody sick for...sorry. That was too much."

I shot her a grin. "No, it's the most animated I've seen you in a long time."

"Well, it's the most you've seen me in a long time. Maybe we have to get to know each other again."

"I don't think you want to get to know me again."

"I'm here, aren't I?" Tracy said. She used her straw to scour the bottom of the cup for the last drops of smoothie.

"Yeah, but who knows if it's just to pity me."

"I know, Bec. I know it's not to pity you. Cuz I don't pity people. I talk trash about them behind their back...with you."

I smiled. "That's true."

She pushed her chair out and stood up, tossing her smoothie in the trash next to her. "Ready to go?"

I sucked the last of my smoothie out of the cup and tossed it into the can with a beautiful arc. "Man, I miss basketball."

"You'll get back on the team next year."

I massaged my shoulder. It ached, even from simply tossing a cup into a trash can, and I found it hard to believe her. I smiled and nodded to her, feigning my appreciation for her platitudes, and we walked out of the mall together.

When we got out to the parking lot, where Tracy's mother would pick us up like we were twelve years old, I noticed Trisha. Clad head to toe in black, except for her hair, which was still that vibrant, neon green, she was handing purple fliers out to everyone that passed by her.

"Wanna come see our band?" she called out to a woman dressed in scrubs. "We're really good."

"I'll be right back," I said.

"Of course you will." Tracy rolled her eyes.

"Her name is Trisha, right?" I asked.

"That's right," Tracy said with a slight eyebrow raise. "And play it cool, because you have a bit of a stalker vibe going on right now."

"Do not," I said, offended.

"Dude, you are totally obsessed with that girl."

Trisha chased after a man in a business suit and stuffed a flier into his chest, even though he didn't seem to want it. Neither did an old Chinese woman carrying an oversized purse, but that didn't stop Trisha for one second.

"I am not obsessed. I'm just interested."

"Tomato, tomato," Tracy said.

"You just said that the same way, twice."

"I know what I said."

It wasn't worth it to argue with Tracy anymore. She would either win, or wear you out until you gave up, and her mother would be picking us up soon, so I needed to act quickly. My stomach twanged loudly with every step I took in Trisha's direction.

"I'll take one," I said when I was close enough.

Trisha glared at me and turned in the other direction. "Go away."

"Seriously," I said, holding out my hand. "Give me one. You're giving them to everybody else."

"Not people who suck."

"I don't know," I replied. "That guy in the suit and the slicked back hair sucked pretty hard."

"Just go away," she huffed.

"I could just pick one up from the ground," I said, pointing to the purple fliers that littered the ground. "I mean they're literally everywhere. Just purple all the way to the door, like a really cheap carpet."

"Fine," she said, slamming a flier down in my hand.

I looked down at the flier. In big letters it read:

The Void Calls Us Home

At the Demon Hole

9pm

www.thevoidcallsushome.com

"It doesn't say the date," I said. "How am I gonna know where to show up without a date?"

"Please don't show up," she said.

"How will I know when not to show up then?"

"Tomorrow," she said. "Please don't show up tomorrow."

"I won't be there," I said with a smile. I studied the flier more closely as I headed back toward Tracy. The picture was grainy and dark, so I held it up to the light of the evening sun.

I recognized it immediately. In the background behind the text was a picture of the flaming eye, the same one I saw in my nightmares, staring at me, in grainy black and white.

"Did you draw this?" I had stopped walking and spoke nervously over my shoulder.

"Maybe." She shrugged.

I turned around and walked toward her, holding up the flyer. "Where did you get this image?"

"What's it to you?"

I stepped forward. "Seriously, how did you—"

"Hey!" a shrill voice shouted behind me. I turned to see a fat, mustached security guard waving his baton toward us. "You can't do that here! Get outta here with that!"

"Damn," Trisha replied. "I gotta go!"

"Wait!" I shouted as Trisha bolted into the parking lot. "Please!"

But it was no use, she was gone. A few seconds later I felt Tracy's hand on my shoulder. "I told you...obsessed."

But I was barely listening to her. All I could do was look down at the flier. The flaming eye stared back at me, beckoning me to come home to it, and I wanted to join it so badly that I could barely compose myself.

Chapter 16

I couldn't stop staring at the flier all the way home. Tracy kept talking to me, but I was lost in my own world. I mumbled "uh huhs" and "yeahs" when I could, but the truth was I just didn't care about anything else except for the flaming eye staring at me.

Somebody, at least one other human, had seen what I had seen in the darkness of my own mind. She called it the Void, not the flaming eye, but it was the same giant hole in the middle of space with light flooding into it.

It meant that maybe I wasn't alone. Maybe I wasn't crazy. Maybe, just maybe, there was an answer out there for me about why I did what I did that night on the mountain.

When Tracy's Mom dropped me off, I ran upstairs and sat down at my computer. Trisha's band had a website, www.thevoidcallsushome.com, which was my first stop when I opened my browser. The home page of the site was the same as the one on the flier, and it was animated. A huge ring of fire stood out against the dark background. The fire collapsed into the ring, just as it had in my dreams.

A few seconds later, the flaming eye disappeared and revealed the main page of the website. I wasn't interested in the band's music, but I wanted to know how they were formed. I clicked on the "About" section of their site, which read:

> *I saw death, and it spat me back*
> *out. When I was in 9th grade, I*
> *was hit by a car, and nearly died.*
> *I wanted to die, actually, but my*
> *body wouldn't let me. As I lay,*

battered and bruised, struggling for breath, I faded into the nothing, and came across the blackness inside my soul.

It called to me. It beckoned to me. It wanted me to come home. I wanted to join it, but my body foolishly decided to live. Doctors decided I was worth saving.

So, I came back against my own will.

When I returned, I searched for the darkness again, but it was gone from me. I researched and found out the name of my new dark paramour.

It was called the Void. It called me home. Into its embrace. But it abandoned me in the darkness, my paramour.

I missed its presence. I missed it swooning over me, so I took my own life…

…or I would have, but once again the Void bounced me back. It didn't want me. It didn't need me.

Or rather, it needed me for a different purpose. It needed me to bring more people to it. It needed more people to love it.

> *My new mission consumed me,*
> *and now here we are, ready to*
> *make you see the light…*
>
> *…or should I say, the darkness.*
>
> *The Void calls us all home. Will*
> *you heed the call?*

I found it hard not to chuckle at the simplicity of it. I'm sure her fans loved it. Still, in its message there was a piece that I could keep. The Void.

I opened Google and typed in "The Void."

Thousands of pictures popped up of the exact image I saw in my mind's eye. It had never occurred to me to do a simple Google search before, but now I was blasted with thousands of images from all over the world that showed me I wasn't crazy.

I was not alone. Far from it. Not only had one person seen what I had seen, but thousands of people had, all around the world.

I switched from image search to the web browser and scrolled through until I saw title "*'L'appel du vide'* - The call of the void."

> **The Call of the Void** is the momentary
> feeling of wanting to end your life even
> when things are going well, like driving
> over a bridge and wanting to jerk your
> car into the water.

It was the exact feeling that I had during that night on the mountain pass when I drove off the cliff. I was fine, and everything was normal in my life, but then my body got cold, and my brain suddenly decided it wanted me to pull my car off the cliff in front of me.

Francis Mane explains that the call of
the void is an affirmation of life. "It is
your brain sending a signal that you
should watch out, and that in any
moment you could fall to your death."
During a study conducted at the
University of Rochester, nearly half of
all subjects experience the phenomenon.

However, psychologist Ursula
Thatcher disagrees. "While some might
find it an affirmation of life in the call of
the void, others have expressed that they
felt as if an otherworldly force pushed
them into action." Hatcher went on to
say, "The horrible truth about this
phenomenon is that we will never know
how many people who committed
suicide could not resist the call of the
void in themselves."

I couldn't read any more. I closed the web browser and
sat rocking in my chair. What happened to me had a name:
The Call of the Void. I felt relief and terror at the same
time. I couldn't shake that final quote from Doctor
Thatcher:

"The horrible truth about this
phenomenon is that we will never know
how many people who committed
suicide could not resist the call of the
void in themselves."

What if my sister heard the call as well?

I stood up and entered the hallway. I quietly passed my
parent's room and entered Mary's. Her journal still sat on
the side of her dresser, and I picked it up. She had

decorated the front of her notebook with flowers, trees, birds, and cats.

The cover belied the dark terror inside. As I flipped through the pages, my sister's handwriting became more and more inconsistent. It started in her cute bubble letters, precise and elegant. However, toward the middle of the book they became hasty and erratic. By the end, I could not even read her words. They all mashed together in a disgusting mash of squiggles.

When I reached the last page I nearly screamed as I dropped the book to the ground. There, staring back at me from the pages of the notebook, was the horrible Void that I saw in my brain. Mary had seen it too, and for all I knew, it drove her to her death.

Chapter 17

I kept my mouth shut all through dinner that night. My mother did not like to think of disturbing things, and neither did my father. They were quite practical in that respect. They acknowledged that a terrible thing happened when my sister died. They did not need to know why it happened. They barely wanted to know how it happened. That was how they moved on from it. They moved on by compartmentalizing.

In some ways, I thought they were less hurt by my sister's death than by my accident, because with her it was a clean break. One moment they had a daughter, the next they didn't. There was a new normal which immediately existed after her death, and they learned to deal with it.

Meanwhile, I was a constant reminder that life was not normal any more. My body was broken and bruised for a long time, and I was still not doing very well in school. I was a constant reminder that things had changed permanently, and they preferred not to acknowledge that point.

"You're quiet tonight, kiddo," Dad said with a mouth full of peas. "Something wrong?"

"No," I said. "Nothing wrong. I just don't like peas."

"You love peas," Mom said. "You always asked for them when you were little."

"That was Mary," I said softly.

"Was it?" She didn't look at me. "I don't remember that."

"Well, you can't ask her," I spoke loudly this time, angry. "So, I guess you'll have to take my word for it."

Mom took a sip of her white wine. "There's no need to be snippy about it."

"I'm not being snippy. I just…you can trust me, you know?"

"I know that, kiddo," Dad said, giving my forearm a squeeze.

"I know you know that Dad, but I'm telling Mom she can trust me, too."

Mom glanced up. "I'm aware you believe that."

"Don't deflect, Mom. You don't trust me, do you?"

She shook her head. "I thought I could but look at the fine mess you've gotten yourself into over the last few weeks. That car accident, your school work. Tell me, how I can trust you now, dear?"

I pushed myself up from the table. "No." I walked toward the door.

Mom hollered behind me, "Where are you going?"

"Out!" I snapped.

"Have a good time!" Dad called after me.

"Rebecca!" Mom shouted. "Get back in here."

But I didn't care. I was gone.

It was bitterly cold outside. The sting of the wind numbed my cheeks. I hated the cold, and winter all together. I wanted to move to California, or Mallorca, where it was always pleasant. My sister told me that I would miss the winter one day when I moved away from it, but I didn't believe her.

"The great part about living somewhere warm is that you can always catch a plane somewhere else and visit winter if you choose," I said to her once, before she left for college in Boston.

"Sure," she replied with a smile. "But there's something wonderful about walking outside and not being able to predict what the weather will be when you come back home, don't you think?"

No, I thought to myself, I didn't think that at all. Not then and not now, either. There was a time when unpredictable weather might have been a nice change, but I learned over the past year that nothing was predictable, that things change on a dime. If the one constant in life was weather, would that be such a bad thing?

The longer I walked, the more the darkness wrapped itself around me, like a blanket. My body was frozen, but I still felt a shiver crawl up my spine. In the cold winter air, the Void opened above me. Its flames fell upon me, and as it spoke, the fire throbbed around the Void's giant eye.

"They do not understand," it bellowed. "They can never understand."

Instead of cowering in fear, I looked back defiantly. The warmth from the Void washed over me, and I no longer felt cold. I felt the heat of a comfortable fire after playing in the snow.

"Come to me," it whispered.

I wanted to heed its call more than I ever had wanted anything in my whole life, but I knew I couldn't. More so, I wouldn't. My sister might have succumbed to the Void's horrible voice, but I had to stay strong.

I shook my head. "No."

"Your sister is quite warm," it said. "She was cold, she heard my call, and she came. You will come, too."

"I don't want to die," I said, shaking my head. "I don't want to die."

I turned away from the Void and ran as quickly as I could back to my house. The Void dissipated from view as I ran, and when I could no longer see it, I collapsed on the ground and cried until I couldn't feel my face any more.

Why was it doing this to me? Why couldn't it just leave me alone?

Chapter 18

I don't remember how long I walked, but eventually I ended up back at my house. I was cold, hungry, and terrified of the Void, especially of how much I wanted to join it in the black nothingness of eternity. When I walked into the house, only the light above the kitchen table remained lit. My dinner sat where I left it, and my mother where I left her.

"Come eat," Mom said to me.

I took off my coat and hung it on the coat rack next to the door. "Where's Dad?"

"Off to bed or watching TV somewhere." She had poured herself another glass of wine and was working through it. The bottle rested half emptied next to her.

"I'm not really hungry," I lied. I just didn't want to eat with her.

"That wasn't a request, my dear. Come, eat. Your food is cold, but then again, you are the one who left."

I walked toward the dining room table and sat down next to her. "So what? This is punishment for disobeying you?"

"Not a punishment," she said, shaking her head. "This is the best I can do at an apology."

I took a bite of cold chicken. "This is a horrible apology, Mom."

Mom took another long sip of wine. "I know this past year has not been easy on you, but it has not been easy on me either."

"I know, Mom," I said, bowing my head. The truth was I didn't know, or more accurately, I didn't think about it.

"After your sister—I took solace in the fact that you would grow up strong, and then—and then…life is very fragile, my love."

She never used the word "love" and me that close together except when she was telling people that I loved basketball. I was taken aback by the sentiment.

"I know it is."

"I didn't come home for more than an hour at a time when you were in the hospital. I thought that maybe, just maybe, if I stayed by your side, you would come back to me."

I smiled at her. "And I did."

"They wanted to take you off life support," she said after another long sip of wine. "Did you know that? They wanted me to kill you, my only remaining daughter."

"I didn't know that, Mom. You never told me about what happened when I was asleep."

"You were in a coma, my dear, and my life stopped until you woke up. There wasn't much to tell. You just laid there, vacillating between life and death, until one day you opened your eyes."

This would have been a good time to empathize with her, maybe even tell her what I learned about Mary, but I couldn't do it. My mother had kept me at arm's distance for years, and it was going to take more than one conversation to bridge the gaping divide between us.

"I need you to trust me, Mom," I said. "I need you to trust me when I say that I'm going to turn it all around. Everything is going to be back to normal."

She shook her head. "There is no such thing as normal, my dear, and this is certainly not it even if there was."

"I can't argue with you there," I said, poking at the cold food on my plate. "So, I'm not going to eat this. Can I go to bed?"

Mom nodded. "Go to bed."

I pushed away from the table and walked toward the stairs. "I really need you to trust me, Mom."

"I'll try. That's the best I can do."

"I guess that's all I can ask."

"You can ask more of me, but you're not going to get it, kiddo."

"I know," I replied, turning up the stairs to my room. I gave her one last look, drinking alone in the darkness, and I pitied her. She was not cruel for the sake of being cruel. She just didn't know how else to be, and that was sad.

Chapter 19

For the first time in a long while I was able to sleep in my own bed without the Void haunting my dreams. Perhaps standing up to it during my walk purged it from my memory. Whatever the reason, I woke up refreshed and ran downstairs the next morning, nearly giddy at the idea of school.

"You're excited," Dad said as I rushed to the table and grabbed a piece of toast.

"I know, right?" I said. "It hasn't happened in a long time."

"I like it," my mother said with a smile.

"Me too. I wouldn't get used to it, though."

"Oh, I won't," Mom said. The usual scowl returned to her face. "I know better."

"Hey, do you remember that thing we talked about last night?"

"Vaguely?" my mother replied.

"What thing?" Dad asked.

"Hush," my Mom said, not taking her eyes off of me.

"Well, I was thinking, what better way to prove you trust me then to let me use your car tonight?"

"Hrm," Mom said. "For what purpose?"

"For the purpose of a concert."

"Let's see," Mom said, stroking her chin. "Should I let a girl who's still two weeks behind on her homework go to a concert on a week night?"

"Actually, I'm only three days behind now." I took a bite of toast. "I'll be caught up by the weekend."

"Oh, well that makes all the difference," Mom said, sarcastically. "I think it's a bad idea."

"I disagree. I think it's a fine idea," Dad said. "She barely ever leaves the house."

"Didn't she just go to the mall a couple days ago?" Mom asked. "And she literally ran out last night after curfew and did God knows what for hours."

"I was walking. That's all."

"Sounds reasonable to me," Dad said.

"See, Mom?" I said. "Even Dad thinks it's reasonable."

Mom sighed. "I'll meet you halfway. You can go to the concert, but no car. And you better finish all your homework by the weekend or I'm going to make you wish you were never born."

"Like that will be hard," I said under my breath.

"What was that?" she asked sharply.

"Nothing."

"Is that acceptable to you?" Mom asked.

"Do I have a choice?"

"Sure. You could just not go," Mom said. "Which would be my preference, of course."

"Fine," I said. "I'll find another way to get downtown. Maybe I'll hitchhike with a hobo or something."

"I'll drop you off, eh, kiddo?" Dad said. "It'll be fun."

"Thanks, Dad," I said with a small smile. Mom's eyes threw daggers at Dad.

The rest of the day went by in a blur. For the first time since I'd returned to school, I was getting back in the rhythm of classes. I completed all my homework during class, and the backlog of assignments were barely weighing me down any more. And since I was nearly caught up with my reading, the material was beginning to make sense.

Who knew that all it took to feel halfway normal was to get enough sleep and not be haunted by the image of a giant void for one night? It's so simple, almost anybody could do it.

After school, Tracy agreed to attend the concert with me, and a few hours later we exited my father's car in front of the Demon Hole Lounge.

"Are you sure we're dressed all right?" Tracy said, looking down at her pink shirt and khakis. "I feel overdressed and way too colorful."

"You're fine," I said. I at least dressed for the part a little better in a black shirt and leggings, but I lacked the requisite tattoos and piercings most of the other patrons sported.

"Pick you up at ten," Dad said.

"Can I just call you when we're ready?"

"You mother's orders."

"Fine," I said. "But…can you like not tell her about how skuzzy this place is, please?"

Dad shrugged. "This place? Looks like a fine, upstanding establishment to me."

"Thanks."

I turned away from the car and showed my ID to the spiky-haired punk checking licenses at the door. I had scrounged up enough money in my room to pay for myself

and Tracy, but just barely. After paying for this
performance, I was totally tapped out.

If Tracy was still feeling generous, she could have paid
for her own ticket, but she refused to spend a dime to hang
out in a "tetanus-injected dumpster fire" — her exact
words. When I tried to argue with her, she rightly reminded
me that any place called the Demon Hole, was "a cesspool
of rabies" and that she "wouldn't buy a ticket to get
chlamydia from a toilet seat." I didn't want her to talk
herself out of going, so I just agreed to pay for her.

"It's not as horrible as I thought," Tracy yelled at me
over the band screeching on stage.

"That's good," I called back.

"Not really! I thought it would be a crack house! My
expectations were low!"

"Low standards are good."

The music stopped, and the band turned to disassemble
their equipment. A short woman with greasy, black hair
and a painted, white face ran onto the stage. She must have
been seventy years old, and yet she was dressed every bit
the outlaw punk as the others speckling the club.

"All right!" she shouted in a shrill voice. "That was
Stinky Feet Machine!"

One punk with long, purple hair and a biker jacket that
said "blow me" cheered from the corner of the bar, but
otherwise there was silence from the crowd, who looked as
morose as if their mother dragged them to the dentist for a
root canal an hour after their grandmother's funeral.

"Please welcome the next band coming to the stage,"
the woman continued. "The Void Calls Us Home!"

Everybody in the bar started to cheer. It was clear from
their enthusiasm they were all here to see Trisha. She might

not have had a huge fanbase, but those she did have seemed pretty into her music. I wasn't surprised. From her website it seemed she knew her crowd pretty well. Everybody in the bar had on either a Ghost shirt, a Metallica one, or one from the Misfits.

"I need something to drink," Tracy said as we walked toward the bar.

I held up my hands. "I don't have any money."

"Ugh," she said. "You are the worst date."

"What will you have?" The bartender had a chipped tooth and bull ring through his nose.

"I guess just a water," she replied, dejected. "Your pipes are clean, right? I mean, there's not like, rust in them or anything?"

The bartender paused for a moment, then said, "We meet the minimum acceptable level required by the health code, yeah?"

"Perfect," she groaned. "That's just what I wanted to hear."

As Tracy waited for her water, I turned to the stage and watched Trisha climb the stairs and plug in her guitar. Behind her, a redhead with a skull headband lugged a drum kit onto the stage.

"All right!" Trisha shouted into the microphone. "Are you ready to think about death, grief, loss, and junk?" The crowd screamed back at her enthusiastically.

"Awesome!" Trisha said as the redhead sat behind her drum kit and picked up her sticks. "Let's do this!"

They started to play, and that's when everything changed.

Chapter 20

The music started slowly, with an aching, melodic rift from Trisha's guitar. Behind her, the redhead tapped the bass drum slowly. Trisha's guitar began to wail, and every note resonated within me. She hadn't said a word yet, and I felt closer to her than I had any other human in months.

As the drums slammed faster, Trisha took her hands off the guitar and grabbed the microphone, letting out a guttural wail, infused with the kind of pathos that most humans don't even possess on their death bed. Her voice dripped with heartbreak as she started to sing.

The world is pain

What we have lost will never
come again.

From the bowels of my soul

I demand something to hold.

Something real

Something true

All good things break

So, I guess you'll do

Trisha stepped away from the mic and grabbed her guitar. It shrieked in her hands as she played, faster and faster until the music exploded against the walls of the club, sending everybody to their feet in a frenzy of emotion.

Punks, whose faces had been locked in permanent scowls, smiled and jumped in time to the beat of the band. A mosh pit formed next to the stage, which I took as my cue to get out of there. My arm and shoulder hurt just looking at the people bouncing off of each other. I went back to the bar, where even Tracy was bobbing her head along with the beat.

> *Come to me*
>
> *My drama queen*
>
> *Together we'll jump*
>
> *Into the darkness*

Everyone in the crowd screamed the chorus along with the band, and my eyes focused on Trisha. She was no longer the gangly girl from school who hated me. She was mesmerizing, like a dark queen, a rock goddess. I drank in her every movement as she shredded her guitar in perfect rhythm.

And then, as quickly as it began, the music stopped, and the lights rose over the bar. I looked up at the clock on the wall, thinking only a few minutes had passed, but it was nearly ten o'clock. I had listened to Trisha play for almost an hour, lost in the soul of the music, and it only seemed like a moment had passed. I felt as if every word she sang was specifically for me.

"That was pretty awesome," Tracy said. "I can see why you have a crush on her."

My jaw dropped. "I do not have a crush on her."

Tracy put her hands up. "It's cool, man. I don't care. Sexuality is a spectrum, and all that jazz. All I'm saying is this is the most I've ever heard you talk about somebody, well...*ever*. So, if you're not in love, you're a psycho."

I laughed at this. "And if I'm a psycho?"

"I'll love you either way, killer, but I don't think you are. You can barely kill a spider. Now, are you going to talk with her or mull around like a wimp all night?"

"No, I couldn't...I mean...she told me not to come."

"And you came anyway. If you tell me you just came here just to listen to her sing, I'm gonna bonk you in the nose. I did not just hang out around a bunch of rank-smelling punks for you to not talk to her."

"What if she doesn't want to talk to me?"

She shrugged. "Then, at least you tried, right?"

Tracy was right. About everything. This was the most I had cared about somebody in a long time, but I didn't even know Trisha. I just knew I wanted to be around her, learn more about her. I found her intoxicating.

I made my way over the sticky floor toward the stage. Butterflies fluttered in my stomach as I approached it. Trisha and her drummer were packing up their instruments while the crowd filtered out the exits.

"I'm going to take a load out to the car," the redheaded drummer said, picking up her bass drum and waddling toward the end of the stage with it.

"I'll be right out," Trisha called over her shoulder. She was wrapping up some cords.

Trisha was alone on the stage. I had the sudden urge to turn away and forget about talking to her. After all, I could talk to her any other time. I mean, walking up to somebody at school and telling them that you came to their show, even though they didn't want you to come, is cool, right?

Trisha looked up and her eyes locked with mine. My pupils dilated, and my hands started to sweat profusely as she sneered at me.

"I thought I told you not to come." She slammed her guitar case closed. "Can't you take a hint?"

"I—I—I—you…were really good," I said. "I'm glad I came."

"Flattery won't get you anywhere."

"I'm not trying to flatter you," I said. "Honestly, I kind of expected you to suck."

Trisha laughed despite herself. "Yeah, we get that a lot."

"You don't suck, though! You're really good."

"You said that already," she was smirking now. "But thank you."

"Can I ask you something?" I said, placing my hands on the stage.

Trisha looked back. The red-headed drummer was walking back to the stage. "As long as it's quick. If I don't help with load out Gwen is going to kill me."

"Did you really see it?" I asked.

"See what?" Trisha replied.

"The…Void. Did you really see it?"

Trisha stared at me for a long moment, like she was trying to tell if I was serious or not. "Yeah, I saw it. I still see it, actually, every night."

"It haunts you, every night, everywhere you go, right?"

"How do you know that?"

I swallowed loudly. "Because I see it too."

Before she could respond, Gwen gave her a little push on the shoulder. "Let's go, lazy! I'm not loading out by myself again."

Gwen had bright red hair, like fire, and wore a tattered jean jacket with a Cthulhu patch embroidered on it. Her plaid red and black skirt was too short, and her socks went too high up on her legs. I liked her immediately.

"I'm coming," Trisha said. "I'm talking to a fan here."

"Is that right?" Gwen crouched down by the edge of the stage. "Are you a fan?"

"Well, I never heard you before," I said. "But I'm a fan now."

"Hrm," Gwen said, eyeing me up and down. She wasn't trying to size me up. No, she was checking me out. "You're cute. Invite her to the after party, then let's get going."

"After…party?"

Gwen flashed a smile. "Fifty-five Tulsa Lane." She reached out her hand and Trisha helped her to her feet. "Now come on. I'm friggin' starving!"

"Fine!" Trisha said, grabbing her guitar case and turning away from me. "Maybe I'll see you there, if you don't have to get home for curfew or something lame."

I chuckled as she walked away. I knew that outside my father was in the car waiting for me. It would take an act of God for him to let me go to a party with a bunch of musicians…on a school night, no less.

Chapter 21

"I don't know how I feel about this, sweetie," Dad said, pulling up to Trisha's after party. He watched as kids in black leather pants piled out of their cars like time bombs, then gave me a worried look. "Your mother is going to kill me for keeping you out so late."

"I know, but remember what we talked about?" I said.

"That you were in a coma for a month and you haven't done anything crazy since well before your accident."

"That's right." I nodded slowly. "And I think I've earned a little leeway, and a little fun."

"I don't disagree, obviously. She's still going to kill us both, though." He let out a dry laugh. "You realize that."

"She'll probably only kill you. And that's why you're the best, Dad," I said, getting out of the car. "Because you're willing to take the bullet for the both of us."

Tracy stepped out of the car after me and waved goodbye to my father. "Bye, Mister Rose."

"Goodbye." He gave us a casual salute. "I trust you. You know that, right?"

"I do, Dad," I said. "I'm not going to break that trust."

"Yeah, you will," he said. "That's the thing about loving people. They always break your heart, but you forgive them anyway. Just…don't get in trouble, okay? And if you get in trouble, for god sakes don't let your mother find out."

I stood on the lawn, still facing the car. "I promise at least one of those things will happen."

"And I promise to make sure one of those things happens," Tracy added.

"You're good kids," Dad replied. "Foolish, but good. If you need me, for any reason, just call me. Do not get in a car with a drunk driver and don't, for the love of God, get a tattoo, or a nose piercing, or one of those studs that go in your tongue."

"All right, Dad. Go. I love you."

"I love you too."

"I can't believe he let you come," Tracy said, turning away from the car. "He must really trust you."

"Or he just wants me to act like a kid for once," I replied. "Either way, I'm surprised, but in a good way."

"I also can't believe you're doing this," Tracy said as we walked toward the two-story colonial house. "I've been trying to get you to party for three years with no luck, and it took a gothy musician to pull you out of the house on a school night."

"You don't even want to be at those parties." I pushed open the front door. "You just go because you are supposed to go, or because you have a crush on some boy."

"And isn't that why you're here?" Tracy said. "Because you're crushing on Trisha?"

"No, I'm here for…other reasons."

Tracy knew I was full of crap. I was here to see Trisha and for no other reason, but she didn't fight me, which made me appreciate her even more.

The party was packed with punks and stoners. The musk of weed plumed toward us as we squeezed through two stoned metal heads at the entrance to the living room, which was filled with too much smoke and too many people. The music was too loud, and I couldn't hear myself think. I didn't know what kind of metal was blaring through the stereos, I just knew I couldn't understand it, and I didn't like it.

"Drink!" Tracy shouted to me. I craned my neck around the party. Everybody inside held red plastic cups, but I couldn't see where they were getting their booze.

"Maybe out back!" I screamed.

I followed the ocean of party goers through the house and pushed open a screen to the back deck. The cool, night air felt good on my face after the stuffy heat inside, and the heat lamps around the deck gave just enough warmth to keep me from freezing.

A skinny girl with pink hair and thick glasses poured beer from a keg in the far corner of the wooden deck. She was surrounded by a gaggle of drunk boys trying to refill their cups.

"Over there," I said, pointing.

"I'm heading that way," Tracy said.

"Have fun."

She disappeared to get a drink. I didn't much feel like drinking, and even if I did, I had promised my father I would be responsible. I wasn't about to break his trust.

"Here," I heard from behind me. I thought it was Tracy, but her voice was too low and gravelly. I turned around and saw Gwen, the redhead, holding out a cup for me. "I'm glad you came."

I held up my hand to politely refuse the cup. "Oh, I'm not much of a drinker."

"It's just apple juice," she said with a smile.

"I don't know how to say this, but…"

"You don't believe me?"

"Kinda not."

"That's okay, but it would be a really horrible lie. I mean, you would take one sip of it and know I was not telling the truth. What would that get me, an extra half second of your time?"

I took the cup from her. "You make a good point." I drank a sip and confirmed it was apple juice. "It's good. A little sweet, but good."

"Thanks," she replied. "Of course, if I was trying to poison you or something, then I guess one sip was all I needed, huh?"

I look a longer sip. "That depends on the poison, doesn't it? Some poison dilutes in liquid better than others."

She gave me a long look out of the side of her eye. "Are you a serial killer?"

"No, just a morbid curiosity with death."

She held up her cup in salute. "Me, too. Hey, listen. You're cute."

I laughed nervously and buried my face in the cup. "Thanks."

"Does that offend you?" she asked. "Me saying that?"

"No," I said, shaking my head. "Just not used to people being so forward."

She stepped toward me. "I see what I like, and I go for it."

"I'm not...gay or anything like that."

Gwen shrugged. "Me either. I'm pansexual. I don't care what you are. I just like your aura and I wanna get to know you better. Can I give you my number?"

"Sure," I replied, pulling out my phone from my pocket. "I'm not really good with my phone, but here."

She took the phone from me and typed in her number. Then, she used it to call her phone. "Now, I know you didn't give me a false one."

"Why would I do that?"

"I just met you. I'm weird, and I might have just tried to poison you." She counted on her fingers as she spoke.

"Damn, now I wish I did give you a wrong number."

She laughed. Her laugh was soft and sweet, unlike her driving drum beats. "That's just the poison talking."

"Well, it's delicious," I said, finishing the rest of my apple juice. "Have you seen Trisha?"

"I think she's over in the corner, like always. Sulking or something."

"Thanks," I said. I held up my Solo cup. "I'm going to get some more poison and say hello to her."

I walked down the stairs of the deck and onto the grass. The dreary and cold yard was made more so as the sounds of the party faded into the background. A cigarette ember burned in the darkest corner and I knew at once it was Trisha.

I was about to have a real conversation with this mysterious girl; a real conversation. Butterflies knocked against the corners of my stomach so hard that I thought I would vomit. Every step was a combination of joy and agony as I walked toward her, and my mind raced to figure out what I would say.

"COPS!" someone hollered from the deck. Dozens of feet stomped down the stairs. Partygoers scaled the chain link fence around the house and scattered to the wind. I didn't know what to do. My mom would kill me if I got arrested.

Trisha grabbed my hand and pulled me toward the side of the house. "Come on, unless you want to get caught."

"Where are we going?" I asked.

"Just trust me, okay?"

And I did. I had no reason to trust her, and yet, I did.

Chapter 22

Trisha pushed open the side gate to the house and pulled me along with her across the lawn. Three cop cars flashed their lights on the street.

"What are you doing?" I asked. "We're gonna get caught."

"No, we're not. All the cops are inside, chasing after the people escaping around the back. They never come out this way."

"How do you know that?"

"This isn't my first party on this block."

Trisha was right about the police officers. As we ran toward the street there were no cops in sight. I turned back to the house and saw a single officer standing at the front door with his arms crossed, but luckily, he was looking inside at the handcuffed partygoers sitting on the floor.

"I hope Tracy is okay," I said.

"She's fine," Trisha said.

"Did you see her leave?"

"No, but she's a very pretty white girl dressed in a pink shirt. She doesn't belong at this kind of party. She'll be brought down to the precinct and have her mother called."

"For Tracy, that's the worst-case scenario."

Trisha scoffed as she opened the driver's side door on a beat-up Toyota Corolla with rusted hood. "I believe that. Get in."

I pulled the passenger's side door open and pushed the empty food containers off the seat before I sat down. Her car smelled like old feet and looked even worse. The padding for my seat was chewed through exposing the stuffing below and the felt from the roof hung down into my face.

"Just be cool," she said as she turned on the car. "Just be cool."

"Me, or the car?" I asked.

"Both," she replied. "I need both of you to be cool."

"I'm cool," I replied, unsure if I was lying to her.

The car chugged to a start and she put it into gear. "There's no heat, just so you know."

My lips were chattering against my will. "That's fine. It just helps me be cooler."

I was patently uncool. Perhaps being good at basketball made me cool by default, but the truth was I was not somebody who could just act the part and get away with it. Unlike Trisha, who oozed cool, even in a beat-up old car that smelt like rotten cabbage.

"That thing you said," Trisha said after a long silence, "about seeing the Void."

"Yeah?"

"Did you mean it, or were you just screwing with me?"

"I saw it," I said after a long exhale. "I still see it."

"You know, not many people have ever admitted that to me before, at least not out in the open like you just did. What did you think, when you saw it?"

"It was horrible."

"And beautiful, too, right? It's the most horrible and beautiful thing I've ever seen in my life. It fills me with terror and hope at the same time."

"Me too," I said, nodding slowly. "I want to be one with it even as it fills me with dread."

"It makes me feel wanted." Trisha hugged the steering wheel. She was talking faster now. "For the first time in my life I feel desperately wanted and needed. I don't think I'd ever felt like that before. Not from my mother, or even…my boyfriend."

There was a long silence. A question moved from the back of my mouth to my lips. I struggled to keep it inside of me, but I couldn't, and it burst forth. "Is that why you tried to kill yourself?"

Trisha gave a low whistle. "You don't pull any punches, do you?"

I shook my head. "I guess not."

"Yes," she said. "I thought…I thought I could be together with my boyfriend again, but by a cruel twist of fate, the Void didn't come for me. I sat in the darkness, waiting for it, but it never came."

She was crying as she turned the corner and pulled over onto the side of the road. I placed my hand on her back and she emptied her tears against the steering wheel. I don't know how long we sat there because the clock on the dashboard was busted, but by the time she sat back up my fingers were cold as ice.

Trisha wiped the tears from her eyes. "If you tell anybody I broke down like that, I'll kill you. You know that, right?"

"Of course, you have a reputation to protect."

"Good," she said. "Now let's get you home."

My father's car was still in the driveway when we arrived home, and the lights in the house were off. I hoped Mom didn't kill him when he got home, for letting me stay out so late. I suppose if she did, she would still be up disposing of the body. Otherwise, they should both be asleep.

"It's cool that you came tonight even though I told you to stay away from me," Trisha said after she'd placed the car in park. "Most people do what I tell them to do, or what I tell them not to do in this case."

I smiled. "I'm not most people." I looked deep into her eyes and held my breath. It surprised me that I hoped she would kiss me, or at least that she would touch me, and I was disappointed when she kept both of her hands glued to the steering wheel.

"I'll see you tomorrow, right?" she said. "I mean, in school."

I nodded, breaking out of her hypnotic trance. "Yeah, yeah, for sure."

I was very good at pretending, and so I just pretended I wasn't hurt that she snubbed me. After all, maybe she just wasn't into girls. I didn't even know if I was into girls. I just knew I was into Trisha. Maybe she wasn't into me, or maybe she was tired. I didn't know, so I tried not to take it personally.

I opened the door to the car and walked into my house without saying another word. I tiptoed up to bed and didn't make another sound. Instead, I just looked up at the ceiling until eventually my eyes closed. It had been a good day, and I hadn't had many of those lately.

Chapter 23

The next morning, I woke up to my phone buzzing. It was a text from Tracy.

> *Did u get home ok last night? RU dead?*
>
> *I'm fine.*
>
> *I am 2, not that u care*
>
> *I do care, and I'm glad ur ok*
>
> *Bite me.*

In all the commotion of last night, I completely abandoned Tracy. That made me a bad friend. There was no question about it, it for sure made me a terrible friend, but there was nothing I could do about it until I got on the bus. Then we would talk, and laugh, and everything would be okay.

"There's a car idling in our driveway," my father said from the window as I came down the stairs. "Why is there a car idling in our driveway?"

"I don't know," I said.

I walked over to him and saw Trisha's ugly, old Corolla parked in our driveway. I looked up at my Dad, who stared quizzically at me.

"Is that how you got home last night?" he said.

I nodded. "Maybe."

"Is there a new boy in your life then? Is that why you wanted to go to that party?"

"Not a boy, per se."

"A gorilla bear, then? They are very attractive."

"Stop it, Dad." I pushed at his shoulder, laughing. "How did you keep Mom from freaking out last night?"

"I told her you went to Tracy's to finish homework. So, finish your homework. Got it?"

"Got it," I said, walking down the hall. "See you tonight."

"Sweetie?" he said as I opened the front door. "Did you have a good time?"

I smiled. "I did, Dad. Thanks."

His eyes were twinkling. "Then all the subterfuge was worth it."

"Thanks again."

I hopped down the steps toward Trisha's car. There was a spring in my gait that I tried to check but I couldn't help bouncing. The sides of my mouth curled up and I was smiling like a fool. I wasn't known for smiling these days, but I couldn't help it. I was happy.

"Good morning, sunshine," Trisha said, rolling down the window to her car. "Get in. I have coffee."

I ran to the car and opened the passenger's side door. Her car was even colder than it was last night. "How do you drive this thing? It's like Hoth in here."

"Better than taking the bus," she said, pulling out of the driveway.

The bus, I thought. I was supposed to talk to Tracy on the bus today and smooth everything out with her. Oh well, there would be other times to speak to her. She had been my best friend for years, and that wasn't going to change because of a silly fight.

Trisha handed me a cup of coffee. "Here."

"To what do I owe the pleasure of your company?" I was trying not to sound excited, even though I was jumping with joy inside.

"I was wondering that as I drove over here today," she said. "The truth is that you're one of a very few people who have admitted to seeing the Void to me."

"That can't be true. It's so obvious from your music…lots of people…must…"

"Some of my fans say they have just to look cool, but I can tell it's not true. I could see the pain in your eyes when you admitted it to me. I can tell you have really seen it. You're not just trying to be cool, or something."

"I am definitely not trying to be cool," I replied with a wry smile. Trisha turned on her own music and her voice blared over the speakers. I listened for a moment before I looked at her. "Hang on. Are you rocking out to your own music?"

"Of course," Trisha laughed. "I'm really quite vain. You'll learn that about me soon enough."

We listened to her band until we pulled into the parking lot, and then walked into school together. Instead of going upstairs to homeroom, where I always went when I got to school, I followed Trisha. When she headed toward the band room, I hesitated for a moment.

She turned to me and said, "You coming?"

"Umm…" I had a decision to make. On one hand, I needed to get some work done before homeroom, but on the other it meant more time spent with Trisha. "Yeah."

"Cool."

I ran to catch up with her. "Is this where you spend all your time?"

"Whenever I can. It's loud and annoying up there. Down here it's quiet and dark. Most people don't come down here unless they need something."

I followed her into the dark. Trisha had a way about her that was intoxicating. I didn't know why she had such a pull over me. I had never been drawn to anybody like this in my life. Honestly, before she came along, I was starting to believe I was asexual. Maybe I just hadn't met my type.

Dozens of music stands and instruments lined the room, as well as a half dozen of the punks from last night's party, including Gwen, who leaned against a bass drum.

"Rebecca, meet the groupies."

"Hey!" a pale biker with a cut off jacket said. "I'm not a groupie, just a fan."

Gwen hopped off the bass drum and walked toward me. "It's good to see you. I was going to text you last night, but I thought it would be too forward."

"Yeah," I replied, not breaking eye contact with Trisha. "I guess it would have been a little awkward."

"I never know how soon to text people. Some say do it right away, others a couple days. I heard six weeks once."

I twisted my mouth up, thinking about this. "I don't…think there's a rule for it, you know. You just gotta feel it."

"That's a good rule," she said, taking a step in my direction. The bell rang for first period and I started toward the door to beat the tardy bell, but the others didn't move a muscle.

I stopped and turned around. "Aren't you going to class?"

They just laughed at me until Trisha spoke up. "Nah," she said. "We're gonna ditch and go play video games at the arcade in the mall for a while. You wanna come with?"

"You all came to school…just to ditch? Isn't that counterproductive?"

"Probably," Trisha said with a laugh.

The rest of the gang laughed with her. Everybody except for Gwen, who walked forward, grabbing her bag with one hand and my arm with the other. "I'm not going with them. I'll walk with you."

"Great," I said, disappointed that it was Gwen and not Trisha holding my hand. As I left, Trisha waved at me with a sad look on her face.

"You're a bit of a nerd, aren't you?" Gwen asked as she dropped her hand from mine.

"I get good grades, if that's what you mean."

"Yeah, I know. You're on track for valedictorian, or you were. Do you know who used to be right behind you in the class rankings?"

I thought about it for a moment. I was ranked number one in my class before the accident. Right behind me was…Gwendolyn Borgen.

"No way," I said. "That can't be you."

"Way," she replied. "Just because I'm in a band doesn't mean I'm some sort of stoner slacker stereotype."

"I never said you were a stereotype."

"I never said you said that," she replied with a smile. "Look, I'm going to cut to the chase. I want to take you out for pizza. I like pizza. I think I like you. We could have fun eating pizza together."

I wanted to like Gwen, but I just didn't feel a spark between the two of us like I did with Trisha. Still, who knew if Trisha even liked me, or girls at all, and Gwen was sweet, in her way.

"Sure," I replied. "What the heck?"

"That's the kind of enthusiastic response I always wanted. Does tomorrow work?"

"Shit," I said. "I have to finish this homework to catch up. I really shouldn't."

"Bring it. Maybe I can help." She started to walk away. "I am smarter than you after all."

"That's crap and you know it."

"Check the standings, my friend. I used to be behind you, but now I've pulled ahead."

"I was in a car accident!"

She was nearly around the corner when she turned back one last time. "Excuses!"

Chapter 24

The rest of the day I was torn between my desire to apologize to Tracy and my desire to avoid eating crow. Luckily, I didn't have any classes with her until the next day, so I rushed to each new class as quickly as possible to avoid meeting her in the hallway. When the day was over, I was tired of sneaking around. I needed to make amends in any case because we had first period together the next morning.

Tracy didn't ride the afternoon bus home until after basketball practice. They had a big game against Hamilton Prep that weekend and I knew they would be preparing for it. If I could get her around a big group of people, she was also less likely to cause a scene. Of course, if she decided to blow up at me then it would be even more embarrassing, but that was a chance I was willing to take.

I walked into the gym as the team was running wind sprints. There was one thing I didn't miss about playing, and that was the grueling warm ups Coach put us through every day.

"What are you doing here?" Tracy said breathlessly as she ran to her water bottle between sprints.

"This is where I come to apologize." I gave a little smirk. "Come on Tracy, you know that."

She nodded. "Public space, less likely for me to cause a scene. I get it. It's fine though. I wasn't going to cause a scene anyway. I just want to hear you say it."

"I'm really sorry."

"For abandoning me."

"For abandoning you," I replied, solemnly. "Did you get arrested?"

She laughed. "Do you think that was my first party to get busted by the cops? I'm not a rookie. I hopped the fence and circled the block. Luckily, those punks may look cool, but they are very, very slow. The law of the jungle."

"You don't have to outrun everybody, just the slowest person."

"I outran everybody though, because I'm awesome."

"Did your Mom pick you up?"

She shook her head. "One of the guys from the party took me home. He probably thought it was going to endear him to me or something. Joke's on him though, I don't date punks."

"So...we're good then?"

She nodded. "Better than good. In fact, I have a surprise for you."

"For me?" I replied. "It's a weird time to get a gift, after ditching you, but I'm not going to complain."

"How would you like to be...our assistant manager?"

"What?" I said, confused.

"I cleared it with Coach. We don't have room on the team for you, but we can always use another person on the bench cheering us on and helping us game plan."

"So, I would be like your water wench?"

"That's kinda derogatory."

"We literally called Harriett that all last year."

"Yeah, but that was Harriett. She sucked. This is you. You're not...look, do you want it or not?"

A thousand thoughts ran through my head at once, but the truth was, the further I got from playing basketball, the less I wanted to be back on the team, and I definitely didn't want to be a water wench for the rest of the season.

I shook my head. "Thanks, but no thanks. I think if I came to the games and couldn't play, it would just break my heart."

"Fine," she said, wounded. "You could come to watch me play, though. I mean, that would be cool, since we're friends and all."

"I'll try to come to Hamilton. No promises, though."

Tracy slammed down her water bottle. "Of course not. Why would you promise anything?"

"Are you mad at me?" She didn't really need to answer that question. I knew she was.

"I'm not mad at you, Bec. I'm just disappointed. I gotta go."

"But—"

She didn't let me continue before she ran off with the team, leaving me on the sidelines. That was the story of our friendship as of late—one of us leaving the other behind.

Chapter 25

The next bus didn't come for an hour, and I wasn't looking forward to the bitterly cold wait. When I pushed through the door, Trisha's car was one of the last left parked in the lot. She was talking with a few of the punk friends I saw inside earlier that morning, laughing and smoking a cigarette. When she noticed me, she waved and called me over to her.

"Where have you been?" she asked. "And what are you still doing here?"

"I needed to talk to somebody at basketball practice."

"Oh right. I forgot you did that."

"Well, not anymore." I shoved my hands in my pockets and shivered.

"Do you want to hear something cool?" Trisha asked, excitement building in her voice as she talked.

"Always."

"Tell her, Darren."

Darren's hair was multicolored, which stood out against his pasty skin. His eyes were a dull brown and a dozen pins adorned his frayed denim jacket. He met my eyes, and then he looked down, as if he was too frightened to speak.

"Go on," Trisha said. "Don't be a pussy about it."

He took a deep breath of cold air. "I saw it too."

"Saw what?" I asked.

"I saw the Void. I drank a bottle of Drano last year after it kept calling to me. That's why I like Trisha's music so much."

"And because it's badass," Trisha added.

"Well yeah, because of that too."

Darren's eyes met mine, and I saw behind them that he was telling the truth. If the eyes were the windows into the soul, then his were tortured with the haunting memory of the Void.

"Not only that," Trisha said. "But he's not the only one."

A fat punk with an electric blue mohawk stepped forward. "I saw it too, right before my Dad died. It beckoned me toward it, but I was too much of a pussy to heed the call."

"That doesn't make you a pussy," I said. "It makes you braver than me, and stronger than me too."

He smiled at me. "Thanks."

"Check this out," Trisha said, holding out her phone. "I started a Facebook group for people in Winchester County who have seen the Void, and there are dozens of people requesting to join. It's like a fan club or something, for the Void."

"I don't know if I'm a fan, Trish." I frowned. "But it's nice to see that we're not alone here."

She smiled and shook her head. "We're definitely not alone. Can I give you a ride?"

I nodded, taking this all in, and we got into her car. She had barely pulled out of the parking lot before she lit another cigarette. "I hear you have a date with Gwen."

"I wouldn't call it a date, really."

"That's not what she said. She said there will be pizza and homework, which is about the perfect date for her. She's such a nerd."

"I don't know. I guess we're going on a date then."

"I think it's great. Gwen tends to move faster than I do, which is probably why she scooped you up before I could do anything about it."

I perked to attention with Trisha's last admission. I couldn't tell if she was joking or not. Was she saying that she liked me too? Was she telling me I shouldn't go on my date with Gwen?

I went with a wry smile. "I guess you snooze you lose."

Trisha chuckled, placing her hand on mine. "We're young. There's time."

I couldn't stop the smile forming on my face, and when Trisha saw it, she smiled too.

Chapter 26

I hadn't been on a date since eighth grade, and even then, it wasn't much of a date. Mark's mom picked us both up and took us to the movie theater, where we watched *The Secret Life of Pets.* It was about as good as could be expected, which is to say it was acceptable but not amazing…which was an apt description of the date as well. It would have likely been better if Mark hadn't tried to put his hand on my knee throughout the movie, forcing me to play defense instead of watching the screen.

Afterwards we went for smoothies at Rudy's Diner. When his mom walked to the counter to pay, Mark tried to kiss me, but I wasn't having any of it. I swerved out of the way and his lips connected with my shoulder.

It was not a love connection and we broke up soon afterwards. Tracy called it the scandal of the century, since he was the third most popular boy in school, but I didn't care much about that. I found him duller than dishwater.

Since then I had avoided people asking me out. When I thought somebody was about to ask, I quickly changed the subject. I never said no, not explicitly at least, but I knew how to divert a subject, and eventually people got the hint.

For some reason, though, I didn't stop Gwen from asking, or myself from staying yes. Maybe I had wanted to make Trisha jealous, and if that was the case then mission accomplished. Then again, maybe it was because Gwen was like me, studious and damaged, smart but dark, wounded but strong.

I decided not to bring my homework to Joe's Pizza when I met Gwen. I was sure she wouldn't mind, but I needed a night off from studying. Gwen was already there when I showed up. She wore a long, flowered dress which she looked uncomfortable in, but I appreciated the effort she made to look nice.

"You look nice," I told her.

She blushed slightly as she sat down. "This is my mother's. I don't usually wear this type of thing."

"It shows," I said. "You know, you don't have to dress different around me just because I'm not, like, a goth or punk. I actually like how you dress."

"Damn it." She exhaled with a huff. "You know, that was my first instinct, but then I let my Mom talk me into wearing this thing. Stupid."

"No," I said, chuckling. "It's fine. I like the dress too."

"Where's your homework?" she asked.

"I didn't bring it," I shrugged. "I thought it would be nice to just talk."

We ordered a pepperoni pizza to split between us. Joe's had the best pizza in town. The restaurant was bright, and the people were quiet. There was nothing worse than a loud, shadowy restaurant when you want to get to know somebody.

"How does it feel to be number one in the rankings?" I asked, taking a bite of the pizza.

"Good." She chewed her food for a minute. "I mean, it would have been better if I beat you honestly, but I'll take a win any way I can get it. Besides, you kind of cheated."

"How?" My eyes went wide. "I've never cheated in my life."

"Um, after your sister died, they gave you straight A's for two semesters." She was abruptly silent, like a kid who just said their first curse word in front of her mother. "I'm sorry. That was rude."

I set down my pizza and wiped my mouth with a napkin. "No. It's fine. You're wrong, though, they didn't give me straight As. They offered, and I declined. I earned my grades."

"Wow." She raised her eyebrows. "No lying?"

I shook my head. "I didn't want anybody to think I was getting a leg up on them. I wanted to earn valedictorian. What a naïve sucker I was back then."

"Did they offer it to you again after the accident?"

"No," she said. "I wish they had, honestly. I might have taken them up on it this time around. It's been really hard catching up and staying up with my lessons. I feel like everything is falling apart."

"How so?"

"Before the accident, everything made sense. There was a place for everything, and everything had its place. I was the smart girl who was good at basketball. Now, I can't play, and my grades are slipping."

I looked down at my phone. The game against Hamilton was starting, and for once I didn't care at all. In previous years, it was all I'd thought about for weeks leading up to it, but basketball no longer occupied my whole life. I could think about other things.

"I just feel like I don't know who I am anymore, and I don't know what I'm doing," I added.

Gwen shrugged. "Well, I didn't like that other girl, and I like this one, so at least you have that."

That bothered me a little. "You didn't know the other girl. You just knew the idea of the other girl."

"Maybe," she said, trying to backpedal. "But this one is still better."

We talked for an hour after that. It was pleasant enough, but there was no spark between us. The longer we talked, the more I hoped there might be, but there just wasn't one. That's the kind of thing you can't force, either.

Eventually Gwen trailed off in the middle of a sentence and smiled at me. "This isn't working, is it?"

I shook my head. "No. It's not. This has been nice conversation, though."

She sighed. "That's never how you want a date to end, with it being nice."

"Maybe don't think about it as a date. This about it as the start of a friendship."

She nodded. "I don't have that many friends."

"Me either. I can only think of one, and I stood her up tonight to be here with you."

Gwen puffed out her cheeks and exhaled, laughing. "That is a lot of pressure."

I stood up and turned around, only to find that friend standing at the entrance of the restaurant. Tracy was staring at me with her arms crossed while the rest of the team funneled in.

"We lost, just so you know," she said. "By seven."

"I—"

"No, it's okay," she said, not letting me finish. She stared icily at Gwen. "At least I know where your priorities are now."

Tracy walked up to the counter and started to laugh and talk with the rest of the team. That world was foreign to me now. I trudged out into the cold, in the other direction, hoping our paths would cross again.

"Come on," Gwen said as she got into her car. "Trisha just texted, said she wants to show us something."

I looked down at my phone and saw the group text as well. However, on top of it there was a second text, sent just to me.

I hope you'll come. <3

I looked through the window at the pizza place one last time. If I went back inside there was a chance I could salvage everything with Tracy. A small chance. I only paused a moment longer before I hopped into the car with Gwen and we sped away.

Chapter 27

I had never been to Trisha's house before. I thought it would be a Gothic mansion in the middle of a haunted woods. Instead, it looked like a normal, everyday house. It had thick Greek columns on either side of the front door and blue shutters on each window.

Gwen pushed open the front door and walked inside like she owned the place. I hung back, a bit more timid. Trisha's house smelled sweet, with lots of bright flowers and paintings everywhere. The walls were painted white, and chandeliers hung from the high ceilings.

A dozen punks mulled around in the living room, where a roaring fire burned in the fireplace. When we entered the room, all eyes turned to us, including Trisha's.

"Oh good," she said. "You made it."

I took a few steps closer to her but felt myself hanging back. "I wouldn't miss it."

"Even if we were busy," Gwen added solemnly.

"Oh no," Trisha said, walking toward us. "Were you on your date?"

Gwen held up her hand, not looking at me or Trisha. "That's okay. It was over."

"Please don't be mad at me. I was just so excited I had to show you guys." Trisha grabbed both of our arms and dragged us into the living room. In front of the fire stood a tall man with a shaved head and a spider web tattoo on his neck. His tattered shirt showed off his doughy white arms, and his teeth were yellow. "This is Walter. He has something wonderful to share."

"What is this?" Gwen said. "An intervention?"

"Of sorts. I mean, not really at all, but if you want to think about it like that. These are all people who have seen the Void. They all met through the group I started."

"The one you started this morning?" I asked.

"That's right," Trisha beamed. "Word of the Void travels fast."

"The Void? Like the thing you keep talking about, the one from our band?" Gwen said. "I just thought it was a weird thing that—"

"It's not weird!" Walter's booming voice echoed through the room.

"Be polite," Trisha hissed. "I wasn't even going to invite you to this since you haven't seen it, but I figured since you're in the band you had a right to be involved. The Void is a real thing. We've all seen it, even Becca."

Gwen turned to me. "Is that true?"

I nodded. "Yeah, it is. Right before my accident. It was actually the cause…of the accident. It looks exactly like the picture on your website."

"And all of you saw the same thing?" Gwen asked. She watched as the whole room nodded in affirmation.

Trisha nodded with them. "Thousands of us have seen it. These are just the ones who could make it tonight to hear Walter speak."

"Why is he so important?"

"Well, Walter?" Trisha said. "Why don't you tell them?"

Walter tipped his head when he spoke, oozing superiority out of his yellowed teeth.

"Because I know how to interact with the Void in a deeper way than any of you could imagine."

"What is the Void, then?" I asked.

"It is a portal to the afterlife, to the other side. A rift in the fabric of time-space if you will. It is death incarnate. All of our loved ones rest beyond the Void, waiting for us."

"So, we need to die to get there?" Gwen asked. "Cuz I am not going to join a cult."

"Not die," Walter said, leaning forward. "At least, not really. We need to enter a state that allows us to converse with our loved ones."

"Are you saying we can talk to people beyond the Void?" I asked, excited. If he was right, I could speak with my sister again.

"That's what I'm saying. I've done it a bunch of times."

"How do you know you're not just hallucinating?" Gwen asked.

"Gwen!" Trisha said. "Please be polite, or I'm going to ask you to leave."

"I'm sorry," she said. "You have a leg up on me. I'm just hearing about it now, you know? And I'm not sure I totally buy into this."

"Fair enough," Trisha said. "But please, show some respect. Go on, Walter."

"Thank you," Walter continued, nodding to Trisha. "With the right ingredients, we can reach out and touch the Void, meet with our ancestors, and do it all safely as often as we wish."

"Did you hear that, Bec?" Trisha said, turning to me. "You can see your sister, and I can see Tommy. We can be with them again as much as we want."

I wanted to desperately to believe it was true. If I could talk with my sister again, she could guide me, and comfort me. She could tell me what to do, and how to avoid succumbing to the Void. But still, I had my doubts.

"Even if that's true," I replied. "It's not really them. It's just the part that remains of them after they die."

"This is crazy," Gwen said, speaking up again. "I don't want any part of it."

Trisha exchanged a significant glance with Walter, then said to Gwen, "I knew it was a bad idea to invite you."

"No, this is a bad idea, period." Gwen turned to me. "I'm going home. Come on, I'll take you. It's past your curfew anyway."

I looked at Walter, then over at Trisha, who was staring at me with hopeful, wistful eyes. She smiled at me. "It's going to be amazing. You'll see."

Chapter 28

"Was she telling the truth in there?" Gwen asked as she drove us home, gripping the steering wheel tightly.

"I don't know." I stared out the window. "I have no idea if they can really talk to people in the afterlife."

"That's not what I'm talking about," she said. "Did you really see the Void?"

I nodded. "It's the first thing that I noticed about your band when I saw your flier. I recognized the image. It's burned into my memory forever. That's why I came to see you guys play."

"What was it like?" Gwen said. "Almost dying?"

I sighed. "It was like nothing, honestly. Do you know what it's like to open the door to a surprise party, filled with all your favorite people? That moment of ecstatic joy?"

"No," she said. "But I've had sex, so I can imagine it's like that."

"Uh," I said, fumbling with my words. "It's like the opposite of that. It's complete, absolute nothingness, as if everything has drained out of you."

"Yeah, that's not like sex at all."

"I guess." I shrugged, sheepish.

"I take it you haven't?"

"No," I said. "I haven't even kissed anybody yet, outside my family."

"You're weird," she said. "I like that about you."

"Thanks, I guess."

Gwen stared intently at the road in front of her. When she spoke again, the words came out slowly. "You're in love with her, aren't you?"

"Who?"

"Trisha." Her voice cracked. "I can tell by the way you look at her."

"I don't know. She is something else. I feel different about her than anybody else I've ever met. Sorry."

"That's okay," Gwen said, trying to keep her voice from cracking. "She does have that effect on people. Just promise me one thing."

"What's that?"

"Don't fall into her crazy. Trisha is a great person, but she's not all there, and she'll bring you down to her level if you let her. I've seen her chew people up and spit them out before. I would hate for that to happen to you."

"Thanks," I muttered. I was a little annoyed. "I'm a big girl."

"Are you, though?" she said. "I mean you just told me that you hadn't ever even kissed anyone yet, let alone had sex with somebody."

My voice was sharp when I responded. "Sex doesn't make me a big girl or not. I've seen my sister's dead body and I nearly died in an accident. By that measure I'm older than most people on this planet."

We didn't talk much for the rest of the ride home. I knew that she wasn't trying to be condescending to me, but that didn't change the way it came across, and I didn't appreciate it. She might have been trying to look out for me, but I had survived much worse that Trisha.

When I got back home, I found my father asleep on the couch watching reruns of *Parks and Recreation* on Netflix. He must not have been asleep for too long because there wasn't a "Are you still watching?" message on the screen.

I walked up the stairs, but instead of turning into my room, I went straight into my sister's. I hadn't opened her notebook since I saw the image of the Void in it, but I couldn't stay away any longer. Walter said I could talk to her again. I desperately wanted to believe him, but how could that be true?

I opened the notebook and started to read. The first pages were hopeful and kind. There were notes about boys she liked and names of dogs she was going to get when she had her own place. Soon, though, the writing started to get more jagged and frenzied.

Instead of words like "hope" and "joy" she started using words like "death" and "loss." She talked about how there was no way out for her, and that nothing made sense. Soon, it devolved, disintegrating into the idea that she could not find peace anywhere. In the second to last passage, she included a poem:

> *There is no escaping*
>
> *There is no rest*
>
> *The Void*
>
> *Consumes*
>
> *Forever*
>
> *A way*
>
> *Out of*
>
> *Loneliness*

Every time the Void called to me, it offered me warmth from the cold loneliness of life. It offered a respite from the world around it. It was welcoming, and inviting, intoxicating even. It was an appealing message, too: Join the Void and end your loneliness forever. It sounded like a wonderful offer, and yet it scared me. How could something that promised something so amazing scare me so deeply down to my core?

In my dreams, I drifted off into the dark abyss. The Void came to me. It was warm, where the blackness was cold, and it called out to me. It embraced me. It wrapped me in its calm.

I opened up my arms and allowed the Void to swallow me into itself. I fell into the black ooze and into the blackness of the Void, where I saw my sister's smiling face beckoning to me, and I was at peace.

Then, a dark coldness fell over me, and I shot awake. I turned on the light and grabbed my sister's notebook as my eyes adjusted to it. As I did, a piece of paper fell out of the back and fluttered onto the floor.

I picked it up and studied it. It was a note written in my sister's handwriting:

Rebecca,

I can't do this anymore. I tried everything.
The call is too great. It's too strong. It
hounds me at all hours of the day and night.
It consumes my every waking thought.

It will never let me go.

I have tried to deny it. I have tried to drown
it out, but it is too much. It calls me to it. It
calls me home. I must heed the call and
return to the Void. I love you so much.

Goodbye,

Mary

Chapter 29

I woke up early the next morning, stuffed my sister's notebook into my backpack, and took a local bus to the Church of the Holy Trinity. It was right across the street from school, so I could head to school right after I finished my business. I wanted to speak to Father Bennett.

When I got there, it was already open, and Father Bennet sat on one of the otherwise empty pews, looking up at the huge crucifix hanging over the altar.

"Excuse me, Father?"

I startled him. He turned around in his seat and when he saw me, he smiled. "Oh, hello, my child. You scared me for a moment."

I nodded. "I know. I'm sorry. It's just that…I need to talk to somebody that's not going to freak out about death, and I thought you would be the most helpful person."

"I deal with death nearly every day," he said. "I'll do my best to comfort you as I have comforted others."

I sat down next to him. "What do you think happens when we die, really?"

"I think that is wholly dependent on the type of person you were during your life."

I looked over at him. "But didn't the Pope decree that there was no such thing as Hell…at least not really?"

"There is a difference between a literal definition of Hell, with pitch forks and demons running about, and the type of Hell that exists in your mind."

"I don't understand."

He looked over at me and smiled. "The mind is the most precious resource we have, my dear. It can be filled with great love and joy, or pain and sorrow. Because of that it determines how we deal with death, and the hereafter."

"What if you are tortured by your own demons?" I asked. "What happens then?"

"Are you tortured by your own demons, my child?"

"My sister was. Do you think she's in Hell?"

"Taking your own life is a great mortal sin, my dear. I'm afraid you would not like the answer I gave to your question."

I bowed my head. "What if you could talk to somebody in Hell? Would you?"

"There are many stories in mythology of people traveling to the underworld and trying to save the one they loved from death. It never ends well for them."

"Even if your loved one could help you deal with incredible pain?" I said.

The priest studied me for a moment. "I am old, my dear. I have seen many, many die in my time, and though it was sad to watch them go, I have come to terms with the fact that I can never talk to them again."

My phone buzzed. It was my mother.

Where are you?

Church

Really. Don't lie to me.

I rolled my eyes. I couldn't believe what I was about to do. "Excuse me, Father, but may I take your picture? My mother is worried I'm doing something deviant at eight in the morning."

His eyes twinkled with amusement. "Of course."

I held my phone up and snapped a picture of the priest and sent it to my mother.

> *See.*

> *I guess.*

> *Trust me.*

> *Be worthy of trust. See you tonight. Tell Father I said hello.*

I placed the phone away. "Sorry about that, Father. My mother worries about me."

"As is her burden as a mother."

"So, if you could journey into the afterlife and talk to your mother, or your father, or Jesus himself, you wouldn't?"

Father Bennett shook his head. "They were here on this Earth for a time, and for a reason. Once they are gone, they are gone."

"And if you could reach out and ease their burden even for a moment?"

"They would not want you to ease their burden, my dear. They would want you to ease your own."

"I don't know if I can do that, Father."

Things weren't any more clear for me, but I had class, so I thanked the priest for his time and walked over to the school. Instead of going up to the first floor, I walked straight into the band room. Inside, Trisha and her friends were milling about, but Gwen was nowhere to be found.

"HEY!" Trisha said, walking over to me. "What happened? I went by your house this morning and you didn't come out."

"Yeah, I had things to do this morning. Can I talk to you…alone?"

"Sure." She nodded, walking with me into the hallway. "What's up?"

I held up my sister's notebook. "My sister…she saw the Void too. She wrote me a letter—"

"No way!" she said, grabbing the notebook. "It's like a family of hyper Void listeners."

"Do you know why I swerved that night? The real reason I swerved?"

She shook her head. "No."

"It's not just because I saw the Void, and it called to me. It was like, it wanted me to join it, and God help me, I wanted to join it too."

"Of course you did," she replied. "That's the whole point."

"Do you think we can talk to them? Can I really talk to my sister?"

"I don't know, but according to Walter, he's done it."

"Are you going to try it?"

"Are you going to stop me?"

I shook my head. "No. I want to do it, too. I have to know what happened to my sister. I have to talk with her. If there's a shot I can do that, I have to try."

She smiled. "Awesome."

My stomach dropped after I said those words. It was as if I made a pact I couldn't take back, even if I wanted to do so immediately. I was conflicted, but I needed to talk to my sister. I had to know why she did what she did, if I was ever to get closure.

Chapter 30

For the next two weeks, Trisha and I hung out every single day after school. She would write songs and listen to music while I did homework. Once I finished, we sat back, watched Netflix and chilled out.

"What do you think your sister's going to say to you when you see her?" Trisha asked one night after an hour of zoning out to *Friends* reruns.

"I hope she tells me what to do now," I said. "I feel like I've been drifting for the past year without her, riding on autopilot."

"I hope Tommy tells me that he loves me and will always love me."

Trisha hadn't been very flirtatious since my date with Gwen. I hoped it was because she was obsessed with seeing Tommy again. She needed closure, and so did I. Once she talked to him, then we could move on into the next phase of our relationship. Still, I took every opportunity to cuddle up next to her, and when I did, she made no motions to push me away.

I hadn't seen Gwen in the band room since she stormed out of Trisha's house, but every time I passed her in the hallway, she looked sad. Then, one day, she came up to me as I was walking to homeroom. "I need to talk to you."

"Then talk."

She took a deep breath. "I can only assume since you're still hanging out with Trisha that you're thinking about going through with whatever dumb thing she has planned."

"She doesn't have anything planned. Walter is the one planning everything."

"I don't believe that at all. Trisha is very conscious about who she lets into her circle, and if Walter is there it's because he's saying exactly what Trisha wants him to say."

"It's what I want him to say as well. He's saying we can see the ones we love again. I don't know why that's so bad."

"It's bad because that's the start of every cult throughout history. God, look at Jonestown, or Heaven's Gate, or any of them. They all started by preying on disillusioned people and ended with a ton of people dead. I don't want to see that happen to you."

"Thanks, Gwen, but I'm a smart girl. I can take care of myself."

"You're smart," she replied. "I'll grant you that. But you're also naïve. You'll follow Trisha anywhere, even if it's somewhere that will hurt you."

The bell rang for class. "Thanks for the vote of confidence."

"I'm trying to help you because I care about you."

"Are you sure that's why? Are you sure you're not 'helping me' out of jealousy?"

Gwen scoffed. "Get over yourself."

Then she stormed off, like some spoiled kid. I didn't need her. I had everything I needed in Trisha.

Chapter 31

There was a time when Tracy and I hung out together every single day. Sometimes we hung out so long that it bled into the next day, and sometimes that day turned into a whole weekend.

Now, I was lucky to see her passing through the halls. One night, I tried to text her, and I realized she blocked me. I went to find her Facebook page, and found that we weren't friends any more. It was as if we didn't exist in each other's lives, as if all the pictures that hung on my walls were nothing but lies.

The more I hung out with Trisha, the less Tracy mattered to me, though. It hurt that one person could replace another like that, and in such a short amount of time, as if fifteen years of friendship were nothing but an old hard drive that you wiped clean when you needed to use it for something else.

I didn't like the way Tracy and I became distant, but maybe it was inevitable after I got kicked off the basketball team. Sports took so much from a person. They required everything you had, and it's hard to have anything left for people on the outside.

That must have been why Tracy was so desperate for me to become a team manager. It was her last-ditch attempt to save our friendship. When I denied her, she must have known it was over.

Maybe it was for the best. She would never understand the depths I had to plunge to make peace with the Void. She had never known pain, or loss, until she lost me, and from what I could tell watching her with her new friends, she didn't seem too broken up about it. I wasn't too broken up about it, either. After all, I had Trisha.

By the third week of me going over to Trisha's house every day, we'd stopped hanging out just by ourselves and started training with Walter. He insisted that we were mentally prepared for going to the Void and speaking with our loved ones. A dozen punks gathered in Trisha's basement every afternoon for weeks, with Walter leading our group in mental exercises.

"This will never work," he said to us as we laid on blankets, meditating, "unless we visualize it working. The Void wants us to come home, and all we have to do is accept it. It will do the rest. Once we are near it, our ancestors will come to us."

"What if we're scared of the Void?" I asked.

"You are scared because you haven't welcomed it into your heart. If you fully embrace the Void, then it will be a nurturing calm in your life instead of a horrible burden."

I didn't buy this. Something was off. Was I wrong about the Void? "What if it's not a nurturing calm though? What if it's a malevolent evil just masquerading as a benevolent calm?"

Walter cocked his head. "I've been next to the Void fifteen times and nothing bad ever happened to me. How does that work, then? Do you think I'm a malevolent evil?"

"I don't know. I don't know you that well. You don't seem like a serial killer, though."

"Stop grilling him," Trisha said. "I vouched for him. Isn't that enough?"

It should have been enough, but I couldn't turn off my skeptical brain. Gwen's voice rattled around in my head every time Walter spoke, echoing my own thoughts about how we were being indoctrinated into a cult. We had a leader with a fringe notion about religion, that was for sure, but the one thing that no one ever said about cults was…maybe they were right.

Maybe the Heaven's Gate cult really did get to their spaceship after they died. Maybe Jonestown really did find peace after drinking the Kool-Aid. Maybe we were really going to interact with our loved ones inside the Void, and maybe we wouldn't die doing it.

My parents did not like me hanging out with Trisha until all hours of the night, but they were too busy to keep tabs on me. Dad's work picked up a new client who had him working all hours, and Mom was on three boards which were all planning spring events, so she barely kept her head on straight.

The few times we talked in those weeks was at dinner, when they would try to extend some platitude or another, or when we were fighting after I came home late. It wasn't much of a relationship, but then, we hadn't been much of a family since my sister left. Soon, I was going to change all that.

Soon, I would have closure, and then things could get back to normal again. Then, Trisha would be happy, and I would be happy. Soon, I would know what drove my sister to kill herself, and hopefully, why I followed in her footsteps so closely.

Chapter 32

It took six weeks for Walter to make all of the arrangements. He invited us to an isolated cabin on a rainy March day. I had to admit, when I reached the cabin with Trisha, it seemed a bit culty.

"Are you sure about this?" I asked her as she placed the car into park. "It seems a little *Cabin in the Woods* to me."

"Or *Evil Dead*," she added. "It's going to be fine. Quit freaking out."

I didn't know what evil we would awaken in the woods, but I hoped at least we could vanquish the emptiness that had sat in me since my sister's death. That was the only pleasant thought for me to hold onto in this whole scenario.

"Welcome, friends," Walter said, dressed in a black robe and holding his hands out wide to greet us. "Snuggle in, let's get started." Fifteen different colored sleeping bags laid on the cracked wood floor. Thirteen of them were occupied by the other people we trained with. In the back, two sleeping bags laid open, and Trisha dragged me over to them.

"Thank you for joining me today," Walter said. "I'm sorry it took so long to bring you here, but this is quite a bit more product than I have ever produced, and my methods are, unfortunately, neither legal or sanctioned. But we have prevailed and are here today to speak with our loved ones who have been enveloped in the glorious Void. As we prepare, please look inside yourself and think upon your practice. Who do you want to see beyond the Void? What would you like to witness?"

Behind him sat a vat of purple liquid. As we meditated to ourselves, he scooped it out into cups and passed them around the cabin.

"This is a special recipe I created designed specifically to lull you into a deep, REM sleep where you can communicate with the Void."

"How long is this supposed to last?" I asked. "How long will I have to talk to my sister?"

"Not long. It takes a while for you to acclimate yourself to your surroundings, and then make your way to the Void. Once you get there, you should have about five minutes to interact with it. After that, you should wake up refreshed and relaxed. I'm going to stay here to wake you up if you don't come to on your own."

"Are you qualified for that?" I asked.

"Oh lords no. It's incredibly dangerous. Each of you are taking your lives in your own hands simply by being here."

I frowned. "Aren't we putting our lives in your hands?"

"Both equally dangerous," Walter said, handing me a cup. "If you are weak or faint of heart, I recommend not joining us today. There is no judgement here. It is your loss that you will not experience the warmth of the Void."

"And you have done it before?"

Walter nodded. "Many times. More times than I can count, and each time I awoke refreshed and ready to take on the world."

I sighed deeply and took the cup of gooey, purple potion. "What's in this?"

"You honestly don't want to know, but it will get the job done." He lifted his hands in the air. "Now, as we drink this, I want you to think of the one you wish to see, of the connection you want to remember, and keep it at the forefront of your mind. Do not fear, or you will be left alone. It is only through acceptance of the Void that it opens itself up to us."

Trisha looked at me with a smile from ear to ear. "Are you ready for this?"

I bit my lip. "No, I think I might have made a mistake."

Trisha grabbed my hand. "It will be great, trust me."

She tilted her head back and swallowed the jelly-like concoction, then laid down on the pillow behind her and closed her eyes.

I stared at the purple ooze for a long time. I trusted Trisha. After a few more moments I shrugged and swallowed the liquid. The great beyond was scary, but I had Trisha to help guide the way. I grabbed her hand and held it tightly. At least this time I was not alone.

Chapter 33

I fell into the blackness like it was a pool. For a moment, I enjoyed floating in the ether, but then I realized I was alone. Frantic, I looked around for Trisha. She was nowhere to be found. The only thing I could hear was the throbbing of a gigantic, beating heart.

I pushed through the invisible membrane that suspended me and moved toward the throbbing sound. As I stroked through, a small pinprick of light appeared. I had to squint to make out, but it was there.

The ether was frigidly cold and becoming colder by the moment. This was not a normal chill. It was as if all the warmth had left my body from the inside out. First my heart, then my lungs, and finally my chest. Then, the chill worked its way out to my arms, legs, fingers, and toes.

I swam toward the light faster and harder, trying to outrun the cold. With each thrust of my arms the light grew, and with the light came its warmth. I needed to keep driving forward, for myself and for my sister. I had lived in fear of the Void, but I would not cower in fear. No. I was a warrior, and I intended to pull through the darkness by any means necessary.

"You only fear it because you don't understand it," I whispered to myself. It was the last thing I'd heard Walter say after I drank the weird drink. I had to believe him. If I could understand the darkness, it would not control my life. If I could find my sister, I could move on from her death. She could tell me how. I desperately needed her help, just one more time.

The pinprick of light became a torrent of flames and as I neared, the great face of the Void filled my vision. I once thought that it was an eye, but I was wrong. The Void truly was a chasm, surrounded by large cliffs. Fire cascaded down every side of the great gulch toward a river of black tar at its base.

"You. Have. Found. Me," the Void said. Its voice was terrifying. "Come."

I shook my head. "I'm not here for you."

I was in the right place, which meant that the others should have been near me. However, I saw none of them. There was only the black of infinite space, and me floating in it. It was a sight to behold, but I hadn't come all this way just to look at the Void. I had come to speak with my sister.

I kicked my legs toward the great cavern. There was no darkness there, but a welcoming warmth which made my skin glisten. Soon, I felt my fingers again, then my toes, and finally my torso. I pressed my hand against my heart and felt it thump against my chest.

"Many don't know why they come," the Void said. "They only heed the call."

I realized that the black ooze at the base of the Void pulsed in time with my own heart. It was almost beautiful, in a way. Walter was right. There was nothing to fear. The Void didn't want to destroy us. It wanted to embrace us.

I noticed something beating against the edge of the Void's tarry face. It was tiny, miniscule even. Whatever it was, it had forced itself against the black tar lining and was bulging through the face of the mighty Void.

"Becca!" it shouted. "Becca!"

It was my sister's voice. I kicked my legs forward and moved toward the tarry face at the bottom of the fiery cavern. The sound of roaring fire was joined by a pounding noise, like someone rapping at a door.

The closer I got, the more I could make out a face pressing against the mouth of the Void. It called to me. "Rebecca?" My sister was calling to me from the black ooze. "Don't…" I distinctly heard Mary's voice but I couldn't make out all of her words.

"What?" I shouted over the fire.

"Don't listen," she whimpered.

"Why?"

The outline of my sister's face pressed against the edge of Void and shouted one word. "Run!"

Chapter 34

"Run!" her voice shouted again through the tarry black face of the Void. "Run!"

I turned around, away from the black ooze. I swam and kicked until my lungs screamed but no matter how hard I tried to move away, I wasn't making any progress out of the clutches of the Void.

"Where are you going?" the Void thundered.

"Away," I said, still struggling. "Let me go."

"Certainly…" the Void said. "Not."

That's when I realized that luring me into the depths of this chasm must have been its plan all along, like a Venus fly trap that drew bugs close with its intoxicating smell and then snapped itself around them, preventing them from escaping ever again.

"Wake up!" I shouted to myself.

I should have woken up. It had been more than five minutes, and yet I was ensnared in the clutches of the Void. It was impossible to leave. No. I had to leave. I had to escape.

My eyes wild with fear, I looked around for a way out. That's when I realized that the fire cascading down the Void's caverns was more than fire. It was filled with souls of other hapless victims of the Void, their arms reaching out and grasping for me as they fell into the cavern.

"Join us," they shrieked. "Join us."

Instead of warming me as it once had, the fire now scalded my skin. I blocked my face to avoid a burst of flames, but in doing so I moved closer to the black tar. I felt a gooiness on my foot and looked down to see my leg being enveloped by the disgusting ooze. It was sucking me into it. It was trying to consume me, and it was going to succeed.

"Join," the Void boomed. "Heed the call. It is inevitable."

I knew the truth, then. The Void was not welcoming at all. The Void was evil, just as I had feared. It was haunting. It was unquenchable desire. The Void called me to it so that it could devour me whole, and there was nothing I could do to stop it.

I watched, helpless, as the black ooze moved up my legs and closer to my waist. But then I felt a great pressure push against it. With a great heave from beyond the black tar, my leg broke free and I tumbled forward. I looked back to see the outline of my sister's face pressed against the Void's skin.

"Go!" Mary screamed from beyond the bounds of reality. "Go!"

A great scream bellowed from the beast and the fiery souls on either side of me dissipated back toward the walls of the cavern. This was my chance to escape. I kicked forward until I crested above the barrier of the Void, and I swam as hard as I could away from the face of it. I kicked and swam until I was hundreds of yards away, and then I came to a horrible realization.

I was away from the pull of the Void, but I was freezing in the barrenness of space. Worse than that, even, I should have woken up by now.

"Please wake up," I said. "Please. Please."

The drink I swallowed was only supposed to send me away for a couple of minutes, and yet, I had been suspended in the Void for what felt like hours. I didn't know how to get home. Walter told me I was supposed to just wake up when it was over, but if I didn't wake up when I was being consumed by the beast, then how would I wake up now?

"You won't, child." The Void's voice was burrowing in my head like a worm. "You are mine."

"No," I shouted. "I will never be yours."

"You have no choice," it bellowed.

"I always have a choice."

"Your sister burned as bright a fire as you, and yet she joined me when the light faded from her eyes. You will, too."

"Never!"

"Life is long, so miserably long, child. And I am eternal."

"Why are you doing this to me? To anyone?"

But there wasn't another word from the Void. There wasn't another sound. Suddenly, the blackness was replaced by a flood of light, and my eyes popped open. No longer was I in the dark vacuum of space and time.

I was in a hospital bed. My mother sat across from me, as did my father, and Gwen. Sleeping on the couch in the corner was Tracy, who was there even though she hated me.

I had made it out, again. I thanked the gods for that. I had been foolish. I had been blind. Never again. Besides, given how angry and worried my mother looked when I popped open my eyes, who knew if I would ever get the chance to leave the house again.

Chapter 35

I found out later that I had been in my second coma. Most people do not wake up from a single coma, and I had woken up from two. My first one lasted for a month, and this one only a couple days.

I had made a mistake. I trusted the wrong people. The only people worthy of my trust were sitting in front of me when I opened my eyes: my parents, Tracy—an old friend I'd turned my back on—and Gwen, a new friend whom I barely knew. I didn't see Walter, or Trisha, or Darren at my bedside when I woke up, or any of my other new "friends."

I blinked several times and swallowed. My throat was dry. "What happened?"

"You tell us," my mother said.

"I…don't think you will understand…"

"No, tell them," Gwen replied. "So they can see how crazy you were being."

"Fine." I sighed heavily.

So, I did. I told them everything from the moment I swerved off the road until the moment I woke up in the hospital room for the second time. Each of them knew a small piece of the story, but none of them knew the whole thing; none of them knew, for instance, about the Void.

"That's some story," my father said when I was finished.

Tracy sat up. "And crazy. Definitely crazy."

"I know," I said, looking down at my hands, the floor. Anything but their eyes. "I don't have…I'm sorry for worrying you all, but I know I made a mistake. I can't wait to go home and put this all behind me."

"You can't go home," Mom said, matter-of-factly. "Not yet at least."

"What do you mean?"

"I mean the doctors told me that since you tried to commit suicide you are on a seventy-two-hour watch."

"But I didn't try to commit suicide. I just told you—"

"And if I go out and tell them that, they'll have you committed. No, you should never tell anybody about that ever again."

"I'm not crazy."

"Come on, Bec," Tracy said. "You just…listen to yourself tell that story and tell me you don't sound a little crazy."

"We just want what's best for you, pumpkin, and for you to get better," Dad said. "Really better. Not just physically, but mentally. Maybe we pushed you too much to get over your sister's death. In a way this is our fault."

"No, Dad. It's not your fault. It's mine."

My mother nodded. "Well, we both agree there. Nobody to blame but yourself." Mom was so much colder than the last time I'd woken up in the hospital. She was mildly affectionate, then. Now, she showed no emotion.

"I said I was sorry."

She stood up, eyebrows raised. "I know you did. I heard you say it. Yet, your actions speak louder than words ever could." She looked at my Dad and the others. "Now, I believe visiting hours are over soon. Perhaps your father will stay with you this time, but I can't. I have too much to do."

Mom walked out of the room in a hurry. Gwen and Tracy said goodbye and then they left, too. Only Dad stayed with me.

"You have to understand, Becca, your sister's death took everything out of your mother. When you crashed, she somehow went even lower. I don't think she has anything left in the tank."

"No, I get it. And she's right. This is my fault."

Dad huffed loudly, shaking his head. "No, no, no...none of it is anybody's fault. You are sick in the head, and you need help. I wouldn't say it was your fault if you got cancer. Whatever's going on in there...isn't your fault either."

"Do you believe me?" I asked him, quietly.

"I believe you know what you saw, and I believe you believe it was real, and that's all I need to know."

"That's not very confident."

"Well, in fairness, Tracy isn't wrong. It sounds, just crazy. You know that, right? I'm trying to believe what you believe. It's not easy though. You haven't been easy to be around these past couple of months."

"I know."

He started to tear up. "Now I know why. I should have asked more questions. I should have never let you out of my sight. Instead, I encouraged you."

"Hey!" I said. "None of this was your fault. Nothing that's happened in the past year was your fault. It was all me, and Mary. It was nothing that you did, or Mom did."

"We just want you to be happy, kiddo."

"I want to be happy too, Dad. That's what we all want. I don't know how to do that, though!"

"Just tell me why you did it, why you really did it?"

"I don't know. I thought it would make me happy, okay? I thought talking to my sister would fill me back up, because I've been empty for a long time. A long time."

Dad exhaled slowly. "I've been empty too, kiddo, but I still get up and march on anyway."

This was so unfair. Hadn't I pushed through? I kept on going even when it hurt to just open my eyes. And hadn't Dad just said they had pushed me too hard? "Well, we can't all be as strong as you, Dad."

"That's not what I—I'm sorry, Becca."

"Can you just go, please?" I said, laying back down. "I'm tired." I turned away from him and covered my head with the blanket. It was quiet for a moment before I heard his chair squeak against the floor. He gave my leg a few pats before I heard his receding footsteps. He was crying as he left the room. I knew I was supposed to be stronger for him, and for Mom, really, for everybody, but I just couldn't do it, and I didn't know why I was screwing everything up so bad.

Chapter 36

An interesting phenomenon occurred once everyone
thought I was crazy. They started questioning every word
I'd ever said. The worst part was, my only defense was that
I knew what I saw, but that was a horrible defense because
everybody thought I was crazy. Everything was in question,
right down to the way I saw the world.

At least Tracy was polite when I spoke to her. She
didn't ask a lot of questions. She just told me about boys
and gossiped about school, but everybody else treated me
as if I was a loon. Mom, Dad, the doctors, all of them asked
me questions, made me play silly games, and worst of all,
they sent me to a shrink.

Doctor Sapperstein had kind eyes and a nice smile. She
asked probing questions and responded to my answers with
platitudes like "how interesting" and "how does that make
you feel?" I would have liked her if she didn't treat
everything I said in such a condescending manner.

I had to be nice to her, though. She was the person
responsible for rubber stamping my release from the
hospital, and thus, even though every word out of her
mouth made my skin crawl, I had to smile and nod to her
like a good girl.

"Have you ever heard of Doctor Thatcher?" she asked
me after a few sessions. I had been fighting sleep for most
of my time in the hospital, trying to avoid encountering the
Void again, so my mind was garbled, but the name Doctor
Thatcher rang a bell.

"I think I've heard that name before," I said.

"I've been doing some research, and it seems like she is the foremost expert in the United States on people with your condition."

"And what condition is that?"

"They call it *L'appel du vide*." Her French accent was horrible.

"The call of the void."

Her eyes lit up. "You speak French."

"No, I've just done some research on the topic before."

"Her practice isn't too far from here, actually. I've phoned her up and asked if she would follow up with you and she agreed. She's running a new experiment, and needed a few more subjects, so I volunteered you."

"So, I'm going to be another lab monkey?"

Doctor Sapperstein frowned, making a few notes in her notebook. "You aren't a lab monkey to anybody, Rebecca. You are a human being suffering greatly, and we are all trying to help you."

"If you want to help me, let me out of here."

"I'm willing to let you out, if you agree to see Doctor Thatcher."

"That will get me out of here?"

She scratched some notes down on a pad of paper. "I'll draw up the discharge paperwork right now if you agree. I don't think you're suicidal, but I do think you need help."

"We all need help, Doctor."

"That's the truth." She nodded. "So, what do you say?"

"Fine, you have yourself a deal."

True to her word, Doctor Sapperstein drew up my discharge paperwork as soon as I called and made an appointment with Doctor Thatcher. Mom wasn't there to pick me up when they wheeled me out of the hospital. Dad was waiting in the car by himself, and we sat in silence on the ride home. He looked over at me several times, and once or twice he opened his mouth to speak, but never said anything.

When I got home, I ran right upstairs and started doing my homework. I hadn't intended to be out of school for three additional days, and the work kept piling up in front of me. As I typed out a report for history about the fall of the Roman Empire, Gwen messaged me through WhatsApp.

> *U okay?*
>
> *I'm alive.*
>
> *Does that mean u r okay?*
>
> *It means what it means.*
>
> *OK...*
>
> *Thank you for asking.*
>
> *need anything?*
>
> *Help with my math hw? I don't get this stuff.*
>
> *Be right over.*

Chapter 37

"Can you explain to me what you saw during your hallucination?" Doctor Thatcher asked.

My father had driven me to my appointment. Mom still refused to speak to me. She couldn't even look at me when I walked into a room and had taken to eating in her room instead of sitting across from me.

"They aren't hallucinations, for one. And for two, you should know," I snapped. "Isn't this your area of expertise?"

She nodded. "It is, but every experience I've ever encountered has been different. Tell me, why did you want to voluntarily journey to the Void that last time?"

"I wanted to see my sister again."

"I see, and this was Mary, yes?"

I nodded. "She was the best person I ever knew, and she was taken far too early."

"I see, and what was Mary like?"

"She was the top of her class. She was captain of the field hockey team and valedictorian. She was good at everything she touched."

"Yes, that is what she did, but I'm more after what she was like, as a human."

"She was kind," I said after a long pause. "To everybody, even when she didn't need to be. Even when she shouldn't have been, she still saw the good in people. She still tried to help them."

"Do you miss that about her?"

"I miss everything about her. I miss having somebody to talk to when things get hard. Things never got hard for her like they did for me. It's still hard for me."

"Now, I wonder what Mary would say about that?"

"What do you mean?"

"Well, if everything was easy for her, then she would still be here, wouldn't she?"

I paused. "I hadn't ever thought about that before."

"Usually, happy people don't kill themselves, Rebecca."

"I never said she was happy. I said she was kind, and that things came easy to her."

"You're right, my apologies. That is exactly what you said." Doctor Thatcher wrote for a moment on her notepad. "What did you want your sister to say to you?"

"I thought…I wanted to know how she did it, why she did it. I wanted to know how I could avoid her path."

"Do you think you need to be perfect, to live up to her standards?"

I took a long breath. "Kind of."

"Even though her standards might have been the thing that got her killed?"

"You don't know that," I said, gritting my teeth. "Nobody knows what got her killed. Nobody except for Mary. She's the only one who knows, and she's the only one that can tell me."

Tears were streaming down my face as I looked down at my clenched fists. Rage boiled in my stomach and up into my arms. I was ready to fight the doctor if she said another word about my sister. She must have noticed, because she took a deep breath and smiled at me.

"Can I tell you about my work, and why you are so fascinating to me?"

"Sure, Doc. Flattery will get you everywhere."

"The Void, *L'appel du vide*, seems to present in people all over the world. Some have a fleeting sense of it, and others live with it for a long time. Most think that it's normal, for the universe to call out to them, but few have ever felt it as strongly as you described to your family."

"How do you know what I described?"

Doctor Thatcher tapped her pen nervously on her notepad. "Forgive me, I am a researcher, and a doctor, so I did my homework. I talked to your parents, and your friends, Gwen and Tracy."

I stared daggers at her, grimacing as I tried to size her up. "Then why did you ask me what I saw?"

Doctor Thatcher smiled a slight smile born from nervous energy. "I wanted to hear it directly from you, of course. Second-hand accounts can only tell us so much."

I let out a deep sigh. "They called me crazy, didn't they?"

Doctor Thatcher looked at me calmly and directly. "I didn't ask them whether they thought you were crazy or not. I asked them to describe to me what you described to them, and they painted a rather compelling picture about your story."

"And what was that?"

She blinked and looked down at the floor, before meeting my gaze again. "That you loved your sister. You claimed that she saved you many times. Did your sister…make a habit of saving you?"

My teeth ground against each other. "Watch it, Doc."

Doctor Thatcher made a few notes. "I'm sorry."

"It's okay," I said, unclenching my jaw. "But yes. She did. She saved me more times than I can count, in more ways than I could ever express."

She leaned forward. "And now you are alone."

"I'm not alone…but yes, I am alone."

"And every time you saw the Void, you were alone?"

I eyed her hesitantly. "I was, why?"

"I have a theory," she said excitedly, leaning forward. "May I share it with you?"

"If you must," I said, though I was secretly as interested in hearing her theory as she was in explaining it to me.

"I believe that the Void feeds on insecurity. I believe the call is always there within us, but we are so busy that we never hear it except in our loneliest moments. Even then, it is faint, barely a hum. However, when we suffer a great trauma, as you did with your sister, and then your accident, it can unlock something within us, something that feeds the Void, so that we become a conduit for it. Of course, that doesn't explain how people just have…something dark in them that attracts the Void, but it's not a perfect theory yet."

"You're starting to sound as crazy as I am."

She nodded. "I know. Nothing about this can be published yet, of course, and it's just a theory, but if I'm right…"

"If you're right, then what? What will change?"

"I don't know. I haven't gotten that far yet."

I looked over at the timer on her table. It ticked down to zero and buzzed. "I will come back and see you again, Doc, if only because you are just as crazy as me."

"Thank you."

I walked to the door, but before I opened it, I turned around. "Have you ever seen it?"

She nodded and, when I met her eyes, I recognized the look. "Every day since my husband died. That is why it's become an obsession for me."

"That, I understand."

Chapter 38

Everybody walked on eggshells around me when I returned to school. I thought it was uncomfortable returning to school after an accident but returning after what everyone thought was a failed suicide attempt was much worse. The hallways quieted when I walked through, in the way that tells you, beyond a doubt, that the whole school was just talking about you and shut up when you passed.

"I think you're giving yourself too much credit," Tracy said as we walked through the hall on my first week back.

"Are you saying people aren't talking about me?"

"Well, no," Tracy replied. "They are talking about you, but they aren't exclusively talking about you."

"They think I snapped, don't they?"

"I mean, can you blame them? Look at what you've been through this last year. Your sister died, you got in a car accident, and then you tried to kill yourself."

"I didn't try to kill myself."

"Says you, but that's what it looks like to almost everybody. It doesn't matter why you drank the Drano, what matters is that you drank it."

"It wasn't Drano."

"It doesn't matter, the masses don't understand nuance or context. All they know is what they hear, which has been distorted fifty ways from the truth by the time it hits their ears."

"There was a time when I would have very much liked to be as popular a conversation topic as I am right now, but now that I've gotten it, I just wish they would all shut up."

"Well they aren't going to shut up unless you give them a reason to shut up."

"How do I do that?"

"I don't know. Do normal things, like come to my basketball game tonight. Watch me play. Cheer me on, like you're a normal human."

"That actually sounds nice," I said, and I wasn't lying. It did. Doctor Thatcher said that the Void was calling to me when I was alone and vulnerable, so if I were to keep myself busy and occupied it would have no choice but to leave me alone.

Chapter 39

I stood outside of Trisha's house for thirty minutes trying to get up the nerve to knock on her door, but I just couldn't do it. It had been over a week since I'd seen her. Half of that time I'd been in the hospital, where she hadn't bothered to show up. I was trying to build up the will to talk to her, but I hadn't been able to.

I wasn't strong enough to face her, to tell her all the things I had to say about what I saw, so instead, I turned around and walked back home, listening to music the whole way home to abate the ringing in my ears. It had been constant since I woke up, but I preferred it to the call from the Void, which had been mercifully silent since I awoke.

I went straight upstairs when I got home, figuring I could throw on a clean shirt before the game. When I sat down on my bed, my eyes glanced over at my sister's journal. I picked it up and started to read through it again. I had taken to reading through it every chance I got since I returned home. It was the only way to remain close to her.

She wrote about everything from the cute puppy that she saw in the hallway to an old man that she talked to on the street. Mary always seemed to be enjoying life, at least at the beginning of her journal.

It wasn't until the middle of the book, when her handwriting started to shake, that she started writing about being alone more. When she went off to college, she no longer had anything to capture her time and attention. She wasn't on any sports teams, and she didn't join any clubs. For as active as she was in high school, she was the opposite in college.

Her entries from high school were always about what she did, but the ones in college, the darker ones, were always about how she felt. She talked about a voice calling out to her, begging her to listen, and when she did, she no longer felt cold and alone.

It was how I felt when I first encountered the Void, like all the hope had drained from me, and the only way to get it back was to go toward the Void. I was so cold, and the fire from the Void was so warm...

The room jolted and shook, quaking as if an earthquake hit it. "I'm waiting," the voice of the Void groaned into my mind. My eyes burned with its image staring back at me in anger, fire shooting from its eternal abyss.

"What do you want?"

"I want it back!"

"What?"

"What was taken from me!"

I collapsed on the ground. "I didn't take anything from you."

The front door slammed open, and suddenly the voice was gone. "Rebecca!" It was my father's voice. "Sweetheart, are you home?"

I shot up like a rocket and ran downstairs. I grabbed my father around his pudgy stomach and squeezed him tight. "I'm so glad to see you."

Dad returned my embrace. "I'm happy to see you, too, kiddo. To what do I owe this nice greeting?"

I unlatched from him and wiped my eyes. "I'm just happy to see you is all."

He smiled. "Wow, aren't you nice today. What do you need?"

I shook my head. "Nothing. Unless you want to give me a ride back to school for the basketball game?"

"Basketball game, you say?" he replied. "I haven't been to one of those in months."

"Well," I replied, "it just so happens I need a date."

He smiled. "Good thing I still have on my coat. Let's roll."

Chapter 40

I thought it was going to be painful to sit in the stands and watch my team play without me, but I was wrong. It was the opposite. The game was exhilarating. Every time somebody scored a basket I stood up and cheered. I even ate some popcorn, which I couldn't do if I were on the team.

As a spectator, the pressure was off. I could eat whatever I wanted, and cheer however I wanted. It was pure, unadulterated joy like I hadn't felt in a long time, like I didn't remember that I could feel. Even when I was with Trisha, I wasn't so much happy as I was addicted to her like a drug. She had the same effect on me as the Void. She called to me, and I answered the call. I couldn't avoid her, because I thought about Trisha with everything that I did.

Not anymore.

That was the past, and I was concerned about the future, in finding out how to get the Void to stop calling to me. I wanted to be left alone. I wanted to have some semblance of a normal life. I didn't know what that meant, but I knew that basketball had a part in it.

After the game, I ran down to the sidelines to congratulate Tracy on a big win. She gave a crucial assist in the closing seconds which allowed Dora Wheeler to sink the game-winning three.

"Well done!" I shouted, wrapping her in a hug. "That was a great assist."

"Please, I just put the ball out there. It was Dora who made the shot."

"Sure, but you placed it perfectly, so she could plant and jump immediately without a defender in her face. That's skill. How did you learn to do that?"

"A lot has changed since last time you saw me play," she said, after inhaling a full bottle of water.

"You might even be better than me now."

"Oh, I'm definitely better than you." She gave me a playful jab in the arm. "Speaking of, how is your arm feeling?"

I twisted my shoulder around. "I can turn it all the way around without it popping and causing me agony, so that's a start."

"Yo, Coach!" Tracy shouted. Coach Glazer trotted over to us.

"What?"

"She says she can play." Tracy gestured to me. "And you said you desperately needed somebody with actual talent."

"I did, but does she want to play?" Coach replied, turning to me. "Do you?"

"I haven't really thought about it, honestly. I mean, it doesn't matter because you cut me, right?"

"Marcy Albertson, do you know her?"

I nodded. "Small forward. Good at defense."

"She sprained her foot in warm-ups before the game. She'll be out three or four games, at least. We need a replacement."

"Really?" I said. "There have to be girls more qualified than me, and who aren't such…what's the word?"

"Dicks," Tracy said.

"Right." I laughed. "I was going to say flakes, but sure. There have to be some who haven't been such dicks."

"I'm sure there are," Coach Glazer said. "But nobody on the JV team is ready to move up, and we need a backup who knows the plays already. It's just sitting on the bench, but if you can do that without screwing up, who knows, maybe you'll get in again before the end of the season."

"Are you serious?" I said, my eyes wide.

"If you want it, yes. But you gotta really want it," Coach Glazer said.

I looked at Tracy, who looked like she was about to explode with glee. I wanted to think about it, but I just couldn't let her down, not again, not when we were finally getting back into the groove of our relationship again.

"I want to do it. Please can I do it?"

"Yay!" Tracy replied, jumping up and down. She wrapped me in a hug. "I'm so excited!"

"Practice Monday," Coach said. "Don't be late. You are skating on thin ice."

"I'll be there," I said.

"I must be out of my mind," the coach said, rolling her eyes. "Seriously, it's your butt on the line."

I nodded. "I won't let you down."

Chapter 41

I spent the weekend trying to cram a thousand workouts into two days. It's impossible to do two months' worth of working out in a weekend, but I tried anyway. I ran, I lifted, and I did just about everything short of sleeping in one of those hyperbaric chambers.

I was sorely out of shape. Before my accident, I could run for three miles and barely break a sweat, now I couldn't make it half a mile. I realized why Coach rode us so hard about staying in shape so much throughout the season. It wasn't something I thought about, but in the moment, when I needed to, I could explode down court because of her training. A few weeks without training and I could barely putter, let alone explode.

After my run on Sunday, Mom was the only one home. When I came through the door, she wandered into the kitchen. She had been avoiding me for days, and I was sick of it. She didn't have to like me, but we were a family. She was my only mother and I was her only daughter. I didn't want a fight, but I was going to fix our relationship even if it meant destroying it further.

"Mom?" I said, walking through the house. "Mom."

I stepped into the kitchen and saw her staring out the window above the sink. She was sniffling into a dish towel. When I took a step toward her, she wiped the tears from her face.

"Mom?" I said. "Are you okay?"

"I'm fine," she said, though her voice was shaky. "Isn't there something you should be doing?"

"No, Mom, there isn't." I frowned. "Look, we need to talk. You can hate me all you want, but you can't avoid me. We're a—"

"Hate you?" she said, turning to me. "I don't hate you. What would ever give you that idea?"

"You haven't said one word to me in weeks. This is the most I've seen you since I came home from the hospital."

She was still crying big, ugly tears. "That's not because I hate you. It's because every time I hear you, I start to cry, like this. Look at me, I'm a blubbering mess."

"Oh, Mom," I said, pulling her into a hug. "It's okay."

"No, it's not. You're my daughter. I love you. I…just don't know what I did wrong."

"You didn't do anything wrong."

"Then why do my children keep trying to die? I don't understand."

I squeezed her tighter. "It has nothing to do with you, Mom. We've all got our own stuff going on."

"No," she said. "It has something to do with me." She pulled away from me. "I have to tell you something." Her eyes got serious and her face turned to stone. She wiped off the tears from her eyes and stared at me intently. "When I was a child, no older than you…I…I saw it, too."

I pulled away to look at her. "Saw what, Mom?"

"The Void. The thing you described. It haunted me in my youth, just like it haunts you. Just like it haunted your sister."

My jaw dropped and I stepped back. "Are you serious? Why didn't you tell me?"

"I couldn't. I mean, I didn't think it was a problem. I got over it, and I thought it was just a phase. Then, when I heard you dealt with it too, and your sister…I have failed you both."

I hung my head. "I think we've failed each other Mom, but we can be better. If we try. We can be better than we've been."

"Can we do that?"

I nodded. "We can try."

My mother had seen the Void and lived to tell about it. She had survived. Knowing that, and knowing I had an ally, gave me hope. Maybe I could survive after all.

Chapter 42

Trisha wasn't in school the next day, or the day after that. In fact, I hadn't seen her in nearly two weeks, not since that day in the woods when I almost died. Honestly, I felt better for it. Part of me was glad that I didn't have to deal with her.

Another part of me started to worry. After all, she had tried to kill herself before. She could have tried to go back to the Void or done something even worse to herself.

There was only one person who I trusted to tell me the truth about Trisha. I didn't want to talk to Gwen, but there wasn't any other choice. We hadn't spoken since before I went to the hospital.

"Have you seen Trisha around?" I asked her.

"Are you still on her?" Gwen said, shaking her head. "Let it go."

"No, but she hasn't been to school for a while, not even for lunch. I'm a little worried."

"Trisha can take care of herself."

"You're wrong," I said. "You think she's way stronger than she actually is, Gwen. She's a wreck. All she ever talked about was her boyfriend. I don't know what she saw when she was asleep, but it could have taken everything out of her."

"I'm sure she's fine. We have a gig tomorrow and she said she'd be there. If you're so concerned, you should come and see her there."

"I don't know if that's a good idea."

"Your loss. Who knows when she's coming back to school. I mean, it's not like her mother's forcing her or anything. She could have just decided it wasn't worth it anymore."

"She can't just drop out, can she?"

"She can do anything she wants. I'm sure she can get by in life with what's she's already learned. I mean, look at what she did to you and you only knew her a couple weeks. She's a master manipulator already."

"What did she do to me?"

"She put you in the hospital, Bec. Remember that when you're trying to figure out if she's worth the trouble."

"She's worth it," I said. "Fine. I'll be at your show."

"You really aren't over her, huh?"

"Yes, I am," I replied. "But I can't just abandon somebody. It's not what my sister would do. She would make sure Trisha was all right."

"And look where she ended up." Gwen dropped her eyes, knowing that she crossed a line. "Sorry."

It didn't offend me nearly as much as it should have. It was true, that my sister had been kind and warm, and it was also true that she was dead, being sucked up by an endless Void for all of eternity, but that did not mean one thing had anything to do with the other.

"No, it's good. At least you're not walking on eggshells around me."

She smiled. "We go on at seven. If you want to talk with her, ambush her later. Don't wreck the set."

"I promise."

Chapter 43

"I can't believe you convinced me to come to a concert with you again," Tracy said as we walked into the Demon Hole club to see *The Void Calls Us Home* for the second time. "This is the place where it all started to go downhill, and we're back again."

"We're back to support Gwen," I said. "And make sure Trisha isn't dead or anything."

"Sure," she replied, deadpan. "I mean, yeah. It would be a shame if she was dead."

"Don't be such a twat. That's a person's life you're talking about, not rotten fruit."

"I'm sorry, but she made you go all gonzo creep and try to kill yourself. I don't have a lot of sympathy for her."

"That wasn't even just her. It was also Walter, and the others."

The other punks from Walter's retreat, a few of them at least, were in the audience for the show, but Walter wasn't there. Darren was, though, and I recognized his multi-colored hair from across the room. I hadn't seen him since we both drank the Kool-Aid in the woods two weeks ago.

"Hey," I said, walking up to him.

He turned to me, looking startled. "Hey, what are you doing here?"

"What do you mean what am I doing here? It's a concert, and it's a free country."

"I mean, I didn't think this was your scene anymore." He wouldn't even bother to make eye contact with me.

"How is Trisha doing?" I asked.

"She's fine. She's fine. Things are…fine. Listen, I need to…go over there now."

He walked away from me, and that's when I noticed that the whole club was staring at me and whispering to each other just like everyone did at school. It brought a familiar feeling to the pit of my stomach. I was used to my classmates talking trash about me, but I never thought I would be too freakish for the punks. I mean, they wore safety pins in their ears, for god's sake.

The door at the side entrance slammed open and Gwen stormed up onto the stage. She grabbed the mic and wrenched it from its stand. "I regret to inform you that The Void Calls Us Home will not play tonight, or ever again."

Gwen kicked over the mic and hopped down from the stage. Tracy and I walked over to her. "What happened?"

"That little bitch. She just sent me text saying she wasn't going to come. She bailed on me! Like it was nothing. This was her stupid dream. I didn't even wanna start a band, but there's no way she's getting out of this without a fight."

"Are you gonna punch her in her face?" Tracy asked.

Gwen balled up her fist. "You better believe it."

A big smile grew on Tracy's face. "Can we come?"

"Tracy!"

"Oh, come on!" Tracy said. "Like you don't wanna see Trisha get punched in the face."

I turned back to Gwen. "Maybe just a little."

"Come on then," Gwen said, heading for the door. "I'm not waiting for you."

Chapter 44

We ran out of the club and hopped into Gwen's station wagon. A few of the punks screamed after us, demanding a refund or some other nonsense, but Gwen didn't flinch. She was on a mission.

"I can't believe she would do this to me," Gwen muttered through her gritted teeth. She slammed the car door and sped out of the parking lot.

"Really?" Tracy said. "This seems like the exact kind of thing she would do."

"You don't understand," Gwen said. "She wasn't always like this. Even when she was a flake, she never abandoned me or the band. Even in the worst of it, she always showed up to practice."

"But she hasn't lately?" I asked.

She shook her head. "I haven't seen her…not since you went to the hospital. I called, I texted, but she always just told me she needed time. I even asked if she wanted to see you in the hospital, but she said she couldn't."

"Or wouldn't," Tracy scoffed. "Bitch."

"That's my friend," Gwen said. "Watch it."

"Your friend is a bitch who almost got my friend killed, so no, I won't watch it. I'm just along to watch you whale on her."

"Let's hope it doesn't come down to that." I was doing my best to referee between them.

"No," Tracy said. "Let's do hope it comes down to that."

Gwen's car screeched to a halt in front of Trisha's house. It was late, but Gwen didn't care. She rushed up to the front door and pounded on it.

"Open up, Trish!" she shouted. "I need to talk to you. Now."

A light flicked on in the second story of the house. A ghostly apparition appeared in the window, behind the drape, and looked down at us. Then, it spun and walked away.

Moments later, we heard shuffling feet on the stairs. The downstairs light flicked on, but it wasn't Trisha who came to greet us. It was an older woman with long, silver hair, wearing a white nightgown and looking disheveled, as if she didn't know where she was.

"Gwendolyn?" she said, opening the door. "What on Earth are you doing here this time of night, carrying on like this?"

"I need to see Trish, Mrs. Burton," Gwen replied. "Can you get her, please, or let me through, so I can get her myself?"

Mrs. Burton cocked her head to one side. "Sweetheart, she's not here."

"What do you mean she's not here? She had a show tonight, and she didn't show up. Now you're telling me she's not here, either?"

"I don't understand. She couldn't possibly have a show tonight. She's been in the hospital for days."

The three of us just stared for a few moments. Finally, I spoke up. "What? That's impossible."

Mrs. Burton turned to me when I spoke. She studied me for a moment. "You're that girl, aren't you? Betsy, is it?"

I shook my head. "It's Rebecca."

"Yes, my daughter talked about you before…the incident. I'm very sorry for what happened to you."

"Hang on, what the heck happened to Trisha?" Tracy asked.

"Well," Mrs. Burton said, choking back her emotions. "She was in the woods with some friends, and they all took some sort of concoction, and most of them woke up, but not Trisha. She has been asleep since it happened. They called me and my husband back from Borneo. I'm only home because I haven't slept in days, sitting up with her. Edgar is there now, covering for me while I try to get a decent sleep for once."

"How is that possible though?" Gwen said. "I was just texting her a couple minutes ago."

Mrs. Burton's eyes got wide. "I'm afraid someone is playing a sick joke on you. It simply cannot be."

All the frustration we had come there with had melted away and was now stone-cold fear. Even Tracy's face softened as we stared in shock at what Mrs. Burton had told us.

"I'm sorry, Mrs. Burton," I said.

"Me too," Gwen added. "Trisha's strong. She'll wake up."

"I know." Mrs. Burton was staring at me. "You were a miracle, waking up after spending a month in a coma. My Trisha can do it too. I believe. I believe in God's justice. He would not take my daughter from me."

I wished I could believe her. I had never seen God, but I had seen the face of the Void. It was not merciful, nor was it benevolent. If it was what held Trisha, then it would take more than prayers to wake her up.

Chapter 45

We said our goodbyes to Mrs. Burton and drove to the hospital. I groaned inwardly. Nothing good in my life ever happened inside the walls of the hospital.

"Excuse me," I said to a smiling nurse as I walked up to the reception desk. "I'm looking for a patient."

"Visiting hours are over, dear," she replied. "They start again at nine tomorrow morning."

"Listen, lady," Gwen said. "We just found out that our friend was in a coma and we need to see her right now."

The nurse kept the polite smile on her face. "Oh, I'm very sorry, but unless you are family, I can't let you in to see her."

"I'm her sister," Tracy said. Her lip quivered as she spoke. "My mother…she didn't tell me until now…what if something happens to her?" She was sobbing by the time she was done talking, and she collapsed on the floor in a heap. "What if she dies before morning?"

"It's okay, Cindy," I said, rubbing her back. "It's okay. Mom was just trying to do what's best for you."

"Best for me?" Tracy rocked back and forth. "How is it best for me not to see my sister before she dies?"

Gwen looked at me, wondering what was happening, but I had been friends with Tracy for long enough to just roll with anything she tried, especially since it usually worked.

"Can't you do anything?" I asked, looking back at the nurse.

The smile had disappeared from her face. "I'm sorry, but if anything happened, I would be in trouble."

"Trouble?" Gwen said, disgusted. "Is that what you're going to tell poor…" She hesitated, and I knew she couldn't remember the name we had used. "Cindy. Is that what you're going to tell her if her sister dies?"

"It's out of my control," the nurse said, giving Tracy a worried stare.

Tracy sniffled, and then her eyes turned up to the nurse. "Were you always so heartless?" She even got her voice to crack.

I knew that her words landed. Sure enough, after a long moment of silence, the nurse sighed. "Fine. What's her name?"

I watched as Tracy pressed her mouth into her thigh to hide her smile. She was a master of manipulation. At least she used her powers for good. One day, she would win an Oscar.

Chapter 46

"That was amazing," Gwen said as we passed the nurse and moved down the hall. "They didn't ask you for your ID or anything."

Tracy beamed. "Well, if they had, I would have told them I forgot it because I was so distraught. I have a contingency for every situation."

We were in a good mood as we walked down the hall and stepped onto the elevator, following the directions the nurse had given us. Once we reached the third floor, though, that all changed.

I was hit with a sense of despair when I reached the ward. On the first floor, doctors and nurses shuffled past us, but on the third floor there was relative silence by comparison. Except for the groans of patients, the beeping of their heart monitors, and the occasional cough, there was barely a sound.

Trisha's room was at the end of a long, dark hallway, and my stomach tightened with every step I took. I didn't want to see Trisha like I knew I would, helpless and pitiful, just like I had been for so long.

When we reached the room, I peeked my head in first. Mr. Burton was asleep on the chair in the corner, snoring like a log. Trisha lay in the bed, perfectly still. Her heart monitor beeped every few seconds to indicate she was alive. Tubes flowed into her mouth, helping her breath, and an oxygen mask rested on her face.

I stepped forward quietly. She was thin and pasty. Her face was gaunt; her hair matted to her head. A single strand fell over her face, and Gwen pushed it back for her. There were dark circles under her eyes, and her sweaty arms had soaked through the blanket underneath her.

"I'm so sorry," I whispered.

"What are you sorry about?" Tracy asked.

My eyes blurred with tears. "I should have stopped her from going. I should have helped her."

"Maybe," Gwen replied. "But knowing Trisha, she wouldn't have stopped no matter what."

"I can't believe she was here in the hospital too, and I didn't know."

"None of us knew," Gwen said.

I reached out and touched Trisha's hand. The second I did, a shock jolted through my body. A dark pall fell in front of my eyes and I dropped to the ground. I saw nothing but black, and then, in the distance, the Void rushed toward me. Trisha hovered there, her eyes closed, between the great fiery caverns.

"I have what you seek," the Void said. "The girl's soul."

"Why are you doing this?" I shouted.

"I want what was taken from me," the Void replied. "What she took from me."

"What did she take?" I asked. "I will give you anything, just let her go."

"Bring him back," the deep voice of the Void replied. "Bring him back and I will give her back to you." Trisha moved closer to the mouth of the Void. Her arms fell backward behind her and her body, levitating somehow, began to lower into the black ooze.

"No!" I shouted. "I'll do it. I'll do it. Just tell me what to do."

"Rebecca!" Gwen's voice echoed in the ether. "Rebecca!"

The Void vanished from my sight, and my eyes popped open. I was lying on the ground next to Trisha's bed. Gwen and Tracy crouched on either side of me.

"What happened?" I said.

"That's what we were going to ask you," Tracy said, helping me to sit up straight. "One minute you were here, and the next you were gone."

"I thought we lost you again." Gwen steadied me as I got to my feet.

"I have a fantastical story to tell you guys." I looked from Gwen to Tracy. "And I need you to believe me."

"Excuse me," Mr. Burton said in a hoarse voice as he sat up in the chair in the corner of the room. He rubbed his eyes and smacked his lips, having just woken up from a fitful sleep. "But who are you and what are you doing here?"

"Sorry," I said. "We're leaving. But I promise, we're going to get your daughter back. You have my word."

"I'm sorry," he replied, "but I don't believe you."

"That's okay," Tracy said, straightening her shoulders and lifting her chin. "That doesn't mean we're not going to try."

He smiled. "Well, I have to admit. It's nice to see some enthusiasm here. Everybody's been pretty morose around here."

"Trisha was my best friend," Gwen said. "I'm going to do everything I can to help her."

"I'm not sure what you can do without being a doctor," he replied. "But we need all the help we can get."

"And you're going to get it," I said. "First, I need to make a plan, so we're going to get coffee. Do you want anything?"

Mr. Burton shook his head. "No. I'm going to go down in a minute but thank you."

"Keep the faith, Mr. Burton."

He sighed. "I guess I have to. It's all I have left."

Chapter 47

I led Gwen and Tracy into the hospital cafeteria. I wanted to explain to them what the Void had told me, but I also needed a big cup of coffee. It was clear to me I wouldn't be sleeping much until I resolved this whole situation, one way or the other, and coffee would be my best friend.

"I know that sounds crazy," I said after recounting what I had seen.

"You can just stop there," Tracy replied. "We all thought you were crazy after the last crazy story you told us."

Gwen put her palms out, at a loss. "But that doesn't change the fact that Trisha is in a coma, and this seems like as good a shot as any of how to help."

"Really?" I asked.

Tracy nodded. "I don't know what's happening to you, and I can't help fix your brain. However, I can help fix whatever you think is wrong, so we can wake Trisha up."

Gwen nodded. "Agreed. I don't know what happened up there in the room with Trisha, but I did see your eyes when you woke up. There was real, genuine terror behind them, and whatever I can do to help you alleviate it, I will."

I smiled. "Thanks guys."

Trisha's father walked into the cafeteria and waved at us. I waved back and watched him walk over to a lukewarm pot of coffee and pour himself a cup. I thought he was going to sit with us, but instead, he walked over to the far corner of the cafeteria and sat in silence.

"So, what can we do?" Tracy asked.

"The first thing we need to do is find Trisha's phone. Something tells me that whoever has it can help us."

Gwen looked over at Mr. Burton, his head tilted down, staring at his coffee.

"I think I can help with that," Gwen said, pulling out her phone. "Trisha always talked about how her father kept tabs on her everywhere she went through some parental lock on his phone. So, if we can get the lock, then we can find the phone."

"So, are we going to steal his phone like we're real criminals?" Tracy asked. "Cuz I have a back story for something like that. I've always wanted to try and jack someone's phone."

I shook my head, standing up. "I was just gonna ask him."

I ambled over to Mr. Burton's table. When he saw me approaching, he took a deep sip of his coffee and beckoned me to sit down across from him.

"Hi, Mister Burton," I said.

He let out a deep sigh. "Did you know that Trisha would have been seventeen next week?"

"She's still going to be seventeen," I said. "Being in a coma doesn't change that."

"I've worried about her every day since she was born. After the-- I'm the one who found her after--

"After she slit her wrists?" I asked cautiously.

Tears streamed down his face as he gave a slight nod. "I found her--and bandaged her up. She was crying the whole way to the hospital. 'Daddy, Daddy. I don't want to die,' she mumbled to me over and over again. I can still hear those words in my quiet moments. I try not to have any quiet moments."

"My mother can barely look at me these days without crying."

I wasn't even sure he heard me. He was staring into the middle distance. "It's hard, being a father. They never tell you it will be this hard."

"I know it's hard," I replied. "But Trisha needs you to be strong."

"I'm trying, but it's so goddamn hard."

"We're going to do everything we can to help," I said, choking back my own tears. "But we need your help, too. Can you help us?"

He focused again. "If I can help, I will."

"Trisha's phone has been sending us all text messages for the last few days. I don't know who's texting us, but I know it's not your daughter."

"Wait," he said, gritting his teeth. "You're telling me that some kid stole my daughter's phone and is pretending to be her?"

I nodded. "That's what I'm saying."

Mr. Burton balled his hand into a fist. "I'm going to kill them."

"I know you're mad," Gwen said. "But you have to take care of your daughter. You don't need to go all Liam Neeson, okay? That doesn't help Trisha."

He narrowed his eyes at Gwen. "How do you know what will help my daughter?"

"Trisha needs her father by her side," Tracy said. "Not in jail."

He took a deep breath. "You're right. I hate to admit it, but you're right. If I wasn't here when she got up, it would kill me."

"Then let us help," I said.

He looked over at me. "How?"

"I think if we can track down the phone, we might be able to help Trisha. If nothing else, we can get her phone back, so that the messages stop. I heard that you have some kind of parental tracker on her phone?"

He nodded. "I haven't had to look at it since the incident, because for once in her life, I knew right where she was."

"May I see it, please?"

"Of course." He nodded and handed me his phone. "The app is called Nanny."

I scrolled until I saw the app and opened it. The app pulled up a map of the area and placed a pin in a house five miles away from the hospital. It wasn't far from where Trisha lived, but it wasn't her house, either.

"Thank you," I replied. "I'm going to put this app on my phone, so we can track her phone."

"Whatever helps you find him," he said. "But please, find him. Otherwise, I don't know what I will do."

"We will," I said. "I promise you that."

Chapter 48

We followed the GPS signal to a house on Mulberry Lane. I had my suspicions about who I would find there. If my hunch was correct, this was the home of Walter, brainchild of the whole experiment that sent us into the Void to begin with.

I pointed at the house from the passenger's seat. "Gwen, you go around back and make sure no one comes out that way."

"Why me?" she asked.

"Because you're the toughest of us."

"Hey!" Tracy said, poking her head forward from the back seat. "Just because she's in a band and wears dark clothing doesn't mean she's tough. I can leg press two hundred pounds you know?"

"Fine." I rolled my eyes. "Do you want to go in the back of the house and wait?"

"No," Tracy said. "I'm just saying that I could."

"Yes, I'm sure you've very scary, powder puff." Gwen glared at both of us.

"Listen, none of us are tough, okay? This is like the weak leading the wussy. Whatever. I'm sticking with my plans, so Gwen goes around back. Tracy, it looks like there's a door on the side of the house too. Guard it."

"And what about you?" Gwen asked.

"I'm going to knock on the front door."

"By yourself?" Tracy's eyes got big. "If Walter is as big as you say—"

"And he is," Gwen butted in.

"If he's as big as you say, then he's gonna bowl you over, missy."

"Let me worry about that," I said.

A light flicked on in the front of the house. We peered through the windshield as a round shadow walked through the room and plopped down on the couch and turned on the television.

"He's home," I said. "Gwen, text him. Make sure the phone is close by."

Gwen sent a text to Trisha's number. We watched as the shadow sat up from the couch and then saw the glow of a phone. A second later, Gwen's phone rang.

"Got a text back."

"That's as conclusive as we're going to get," I replied. "All right, we're doing my plan, okay?"

"Whatever," Gwen said, pushing the car door open.

"Is there a signal?" Tracy asked as we walked toward the house together.

"A signal?"

"In case things go wrong."

"Yeah," I said. "I'll scream. Real loud. If I do, you come running."

"Got it." She headed to the side of the house.

I stepped up the concrete steps to the front door and held my breath. Then, I exhaled slowly and carefully. I had no idea what my plan was.

Not having a plan had never stopped me before. I took another slow breath and knocked on the door.

"Go away!" a man's voice bellowed.

I didn't reply, except to knock louder the second time.

"Didn't you hear me?"

The third time I slammed my fist on the door as hard as I could, and when I was done the couch finally creaked, and a loud groan escaped the mouth of whomever was inside as they waddled to the door. The lock flipped and the door flung open. Sure enough, there was Walter, his gut poking out of a ripped Iron Maiden t-shirt.

"What?" he shouted.

"We need to talk," I said as his eyes settled on me. "Do you have Trisha's phone?"

Immediately, Walter's eyes went wide. His body jerked around, and he flailed his arms toward the back of the house. "I'm not home right now!"

Walter lumbered through the rooms and I gave chase. The house wasn't large, and I was halfway to the kitchen after only a couple of steps. As I ran, a chirping sound echoed through the house, like a bird was trapped next to a loudspeaker.

"You can't come in here!" Walter turned to the back door. "That's trespassing!"

I didn't care that I was breaking the law, and I doubted that Walter would tattle on me to the authorities, given everything I knew about him. On my way down the hallway, a blue light from the bedroom caught my eye. My head naturally cocked toward the light, and my jaw dropped to the floor.

I stopped dead in my tracks. In front of me, hovering in the air, was a teenage boy with hollow eyes and a translucent body. A blue glow emanated from him as he hovered, giving off a low hum.

"Ow!" Walter screamed from the kitchen and I heard a loud thump on the floor. "What did you do that for?"

"Shut up!" Gwen shouted. "Becca. You all right?"

"I'm fine," I said, stepping inside the room toward the blue light. It moved away from me, toward the wall.

Every time I stepped forward, it moved backward. I held up my hands. "I'm not going to hurt you."

"What are you doing back—" Gwen said as she came down the hallway. When she came into the bedroom, she stopped cold. "Thomas?"

"You know who this is?"

"Of course I do," she said, not taking her eyes off of the blue apparition. "That is Trisha's boyfriend."

Chapter 49

Gwen and I walked back to the kitchen, where Walter was on the floor writhing in pain. "I can't believe you did that!"

"Oh, come on, you big baby," Gwen said. "It doesn't hurt that bad."

"What did you do to him?"

She shrugged. "I kicked him in the balls. It's my only self-defense move."

"Effective." I nodded, staring at the huge man on the linoleum.

"You punk!" he shouted, rocking from one side to the other. "I'm gonna kill you!"

Gwen knelt next to him. "That's not very nice."

"It's fine," I said. "He already tried once and failed."

"I didn't try to kill you!" he shouted. "I was trying to help you get closure!"

"Whatever. This isn't about me. We need to talk to you about Trisha."

Walter nodded, still grimacing and panting. "Can you get me a bag of peas from the freezer? Please."

I pulled a bag of peas from the freezer and threw it at him. He sighed with relief when he placed them on his crotch.

"Thank you."

"You should thank her," Gwen said. "It's more courtesy than I would have given you."

"You stole Trisha's phone," I said to him. "Why?"

He shook his head, his eyes closed. "I don't know. I don't know."

"Dude," Gwen replied. "Don't make me hurt you."

"All right! I didn't steal it, though. I just kind of ended up with it after the accident."

"Did you know Trisha wouldn't wake up?"

"Of course not!" he shouted. "Everybody else woke up. Everybody, except for you and Trisha. After that nobody would even talk to me."

"So what? You just left her there."

"I went to drop you off at the hospital, and when I came back, she was gone."

Gwen scratched her head. "Why didn't you take both of them?"

"Have you ever tried to carry an unconscious girl to a car?"

"No," Gwen said. "Thank god."

"It's like deadlifting a tractor," he said, turning to me. "By the time I got you to the car I thought I was going to have a heart attack. So, I figured I would drop you off and come back for her."

"That's stupid," I replied.

"All of this is stupid." He took a deep breath. "When I got back, she was gone. I didn't know where she went. All that was left was her phone, and that…that blue thing. It's been following me ever since."

"The ghost?" I asked.

"Who cares about the stupid ghost?" Gwen said, cracking her knuckles. "Who took Trisha to the hospital then, if it wasn't you?"

"I didn't know what happened at the time, but I learned later that it was Darren. He came back to find me, and he saw her lying on the ground in a coma. He took her to the hospital. I didn't learn that until this morning, after I had already been texting with people from Trisha's phone for days, pretending she was all right. I couldn't just stop without people figuring out what happened."

"That's stupid," I scoffed. "Eventually everybody was going to find out. It was only a matter of time. Hell, her parents were already at the hospital. This is the dumbest plan I've ever heard!"

"I know!" Walter shouted. "I'm not in my rational mind, okay? I've never had to deal with somebody maybe dying because of something I did."

"Why didn't you throw the phone away? It's like, proof you committed a felony."

"It wasn't supposed to be a felony!" Walter said, rubbing his temples. "Nobody was supposed to get hurt."

"Then why did you feed them poison?" Gwen snarled at him. "Seems like you were asking for trouble."

"It wasn't poison!" Walter said. "It was supposed to help. I was just trying to help."

I threw my hands in the air, shouting. "Well, you didn't. Now, Trisha's in the hospital, clinging to life, because of you."

Walter sat up and leaned against the kitchen counter. "I know. I'm sorry about that. She can't die, though. If she dies, I'm going away for murder."

"You're goddamn right you are!" Gwen shouted.

"She's not going to die," I said quietly. "When I touched her, I had a vision."

"What kind of vision?" Walter asked.

"Of the Void. It had Trisha and was holding her soul hostage. It was demanding I give something back before the Void let her go. I didn't know what it was talking about…until now."

"What?" Gwen said. "You think it wants Thomas?"

"It would make sense, wouldn't it? I mean, something must have happened that let Thomas come back to the real world, and it pissed off the Void pretty bad."

"The Void doesn't get pissed off," Walter scoffed. "It's a benevolent deity."

"That's garbage," I snapped. "It's pure evil. But that doesn't matter. Walter, how do you return that thing to the Void?"

"I don't know!" Walter's voice cracked. "I don't even know how it got here in the first place. How would I know how to get it back to the Void?"

"I thought you were the expert on the Void. That's what you've been saying!"

He hung his head. "Yeah, well…people lie."

"Boy howdy, you got that right," Gwen said.

"I'm not surprised you're a liar." I knelt down next to Walter. "But I need your help to figure this out. Otherwise, Trisha's gonna die and you're gonna go to jail."

"I can't go to jail." Walter covered his face with his hands.

"Then you need to help me."

"Fine," he said. "I'll start doing some research and see if there's anything I can figure out."

"Good." I got to my feet.

"What do the rest of us do?" Gwen asked.

"I have some ideas," I said. "But they're gonna take some leg work. Care to take a drive tomorrow after school?"

Before Gwen could respond, Tracy stumbled through the door. She looked at me, and then Walter, then back to me. "What is going on in here?"

"We're hatching a scheme," Gwen said.

"What happened to screaming for help?" Tracy asked. "I've been standing at that side door like a moron."

I shrugged. "I guess we didn't need it."

"Yeah," she said. "But I missed out on all the fun."

"It wasn't that much fun," Gwen said. "I got to hit old Walter here in the balls, though."

"Aw man," Tracy said, throwing up her hands. "I would have liked to see that."

"Next time." I smiled. "Promise."

Chapter 50

I was smart, but there were limits to my knowledge. I had no idea how to sacrifice Thomas's soul so that Trisha could come back from the brink of death. Seemed like a pretty tall order. That was the kind of thing religion was good for, though.

Once again, I got up early and took the bus to the church, and once again I found Father Bennett inside preparing the church for the day. This time he was at the altar, unfolding the linens for morning mass. Before I walked up and talked to him, I took a picture of the church and sent it to my mother, time-stamped, so she wouldn't worry.

The priest smiled at me as I approached the altar. "Back again? I'm happy that you have found a new appreciation for the church."

"I've been going through some things these days, Father. I'm hoping you can help me."

Father Bennett stepped down from the altar and walked toward me. "If I can do so, I certainly will."

"Do you believe we have a soul?"

"Of course, I do, my dear."

"What is the soul, then?"

"Oh, I've read many explanations over the years. The one I like best is that the soul is our everlasting spirit, that which carries on after our corporeal body dies. It is the piece of us that is closest to God. Some even say it is the spark of God himself."

"And can it be separated from your body during your life?"

"Well, we have seen it happen with out of body experiences on many occasions. People have come back from death and relayed experiences of being outside their bodies looking down on it, and that is the closest I have found to proof of such a thing. Frankly, it is all the proof I need."

"How long can somebody survive without their soul, Father?"

"These are very…advanced questions. Are you considering a career in the clergy, my dear?"

I shook my head. "No, Father. I am just a curious party."

Father Bennett stared at me for a long moment. "I wish I had a good answer, Rebecca, but I'm afraid I don't. It might be a minute, an hour, or a thousand years."

"Do you know how to return a soul to its body?"

Another shake of his head. "I have not come across any research on that in all my years. However, some might exist."

"Thank you, Father," I replied. "Can I ask you something else?"

"You can ask me as many questions as you want. Most people don't have even a passing interest in this topic, but I have always found it fascinating."

"Let's say, hypothetically, the only way to save somebody you loved was to send somebody else to Hell forever. What would you do?"

Father stopped in his tracks. "I'm not sure, but this is really about what you would do, isn't it?"

"I don't know what I should do. That's why I'm here."

"Well, then. I suppose the question you have to ask yourself is which is greater, the good you do for your friend or the bad you do to save her?"

"I don't know, Father. That's why I'm asking you."

The priest laughed. "Yes, that is what people often say to me. They want me to give them a definitive answer, but that is not within the purview of my job. My job is to get them to see the right answer within themselves."

"Well, then I think you failed, Father, because I'm just as confused now as when I came to you."

"Give it time, the right answer will come to you."

"I hope so."

Chapter 51

Basketball practice was hard when you were too tired to keep your eyes open. I got hit in the head at least three times every afternoon for the rest of the week, but that wasn't the worst part. The worst part was that I wasn't improving as much as I expected, and certainly not as much as Coach demanded.

Part of me hoped that I would step back onto the court and everything would be like it was before the accident, but it looked like I had lost my touch. I missed easy passes, and even layups were a problem for me. Literally, a layup. When somebody calls something easy, what do they say?

It's a layup.

"You'll get it," Tracy told me every time I screwed up. "I believe in you."

I was sick of people believing in me. When people believe in you, it's that much easier to let them down. If people don't have any expectations of you, then it's a lot easier to meet them.

"You just need a good night's sleep," Tracy said after a particularly bad shot. The ball didn't come three feet from the net.

"How can I sleep, Trace?" I said. "Every time I close my eyes, images of the Void jolt me back awake."

"Well, you have to think of something." Tracy pointed to the coach. "If you don't pull it together, then she's gonna cut you again."

"I'm working as hard as I can, Tracy," I said. "I'm overclocking my CPU by a thousand percent to make sure I can do everything for everybody."

"You don't have to do everything, Bec," Tracy said, watching me attempt another three pointer. It clanged off the backboard. "Better."

"I just need to get this Trisha situation figured out," I said. "Once she wakes up, I can go back to sleep, and everything will go back to normal."

"Are you sure about that?" she asked. "No matter what you do, the Void is still going to be out there, waiting for you."

"I can't think like that," I said. "I need to handle one thing first."

"Good idea!" Coach said, walking by on her way to the sideline. "How about handling getting the ball into the net!"

"On it, Coach!" I said, taking another shot. The ball rattled around the rim before falling out.

"Your friend might think trying is good enough, but I need results! Results win games!"

"Yes, Coach!" I turned to Tracy. "I need your help."

"Whatever I can do."

"The Burtons aren't giving me any updates on Trisha's condition. I need you to go there after practice every day until I tell you otherwise and spy on Trisha for me. Make sure nothing happens to her."

"That sounds boring," Tracy replied.

"Super boring."

She sighed. "I hate Trisha."

"Do you hate her so much you want her to be eaten up by a malevolent beast from the great beyond?"

"Yes?" she said, questioning herself.

I fired off another shot. This one fell through the basket with a swish. It was the perfect shot. I hadn't hit a perfect shot since I'd come back to the team.

"Nice work!" Coach shouted. "Again!"

"Yes, ma'am!" I dribbled the ball. "I don't think that's true, Tracy. And even if it's true, do it as a favor to me."

"You owe me so many favors," Tracy said, taking a shot with her ball.

"They'll be repaid, with interest, once this is all figured out."

"Fine," Tracy said. "I'll help, but you better step up your game. I expect to win state this year, and you're my secret weapon."

"You're my secret weapon, too, buddy." I fired off another shot and it fell through the hoop for a second time.

"One more like that and you've got yourself a streak going," she said, stealing the ball from me and driving to the basket.

"I won't let it go to my head."

"Sure, you will!" Tracy laughed. "That's what I love about you. You let everything go to your head. What I hate about you, too. Now come on, drive the basket."

Chapter 52

"Did you find anything?" I asked, sitting on the bed in Walter's room after basketball practice. I smelled terrible, but my odor was masked by the smelly clothes and half-eaten food strewn across his room. He never cleaned, and rarely ever showered. His house was a sty, and I would not have been caught dead there if it wasn't where Thomas's ghost was stationed.

"Nothing that we don't already know," Walter replied from his computer chair. He was searching the internet for more information on the Void. "There's surprisingly little information about our connection to the afterlife."

Thomas's ghost floated in the center of the room, hovering back and forth as if it were anxiously pacing across the room. I hadn't seen the ghost change its face from worried consternation since we'd found him.

"What do we know so far then?" I asked.

"We know the Void is some sort of being that sucks in souls and that exists beyond a great expanse of darkness. We know that nearly half the population has heard the call of the Void before. We know that it has Trisha, and we know it hounds you relentlessly."

"That's not much," I said. "Do you know Doctor Thatcher?"

He nodded. "She's one of the foremost experts on the Void in the world."

Gwen raised her hand. "Frankly, I think we are the foremost experts on the Void in the world," she said.

"Fair enough," Walter replied. "But she is one of the greatest academic minds on the topic."

"I saw her a couple of times after I came back from the Void. I wonder if she would know anything else about how to interact with it. Maybe she can put us on the right path."

"It wouldn't hurt to ask."

Gwen hadn't taken her eyes off Thomas's ghost since we arrived at Walter's house that night. He hadn't said a word to us since we discovered him in Walter's house, and it was truly one of the creepiest things about him, which is saying something, since he was a non-corporeal ghost.

"What do you think Tommy's ghost wants?" Gwen said. "Do you think it wants to go back?"

"No," I said, shaking my head. "But he doesn't have a choice. He's dead and Trisha is alive."

"I know. It's just a shame is all," Gwen said. "Why do you think it's not talking?"

"I don't know," Walter said. He was looking at something on his computer. "Why would souls be able to talk? They don't have voice boxes."

"Touché," Gwen replied.

I leaned against the wall. I wanted so badly to lay back in Walter's bed and fall sleep, but I couldn't, not until we figured it out and sent Thomas back to the Void. I needed to sever my connection with it. Then, and only then, could I sleep soundly again.

I looked at Walter, suddenly. "But you were there, weren't you? You told me that you spoke to your ancestors dozens of times."

"About that," Walter said, turning around. "I have a confession to make."

Gwen sat up. "This can't be good."

"I never actually talked to my ancestors. That was all a lie."

"Excuse me?" I said, nostrils flaring. "Are you saying you had us ingest poison, poison that sent me and Trisha into the hospital, poison that left Trisha's soul in the possession of the Void, and you hadn't even tried it before?"

"No," Walter said. "That's not what I'm saying. I used the potion I made a dozen times, but I could never will myself to swim closer out of the blackness toward the Void. I always stayed at a distance."

"You were the one who told me the Void was friendly!" I shouted.

"That's just a thing you say!" Walter said. "It's horrifying. It was horrifying. I wanted it to be kind. I so desperately wanted not to be afraid, but every time I went to visit it…I couldn't."

"Why would you want to visit it anyway?" Gwen asked. "It doesn't make any sense. From everything I understand, the Void is a horrible being of indescribable power."

"I didn't know it was horrible, then," Walter replied. "After my mother died, I found a notebook that she wrote in every day, and she mentioned the Void. She drew paintings of it. She sketched it. She said it called to her. She said it was kind to her."

"Did she kill herself?"

"No," Walter replied. "She died of cancer, just like most of the women in my family, and the men. Just like I will, too." Walter sighed deeply. "I wanted to see what it was like, to die, to see what she saw, to ask her if it was painful. So maybe I wouldn't be so scared when it took me, too." He was crying when he finished. "Sounds stupid, I know."

I shook my head. "That doesn't sound stupid. Convincing a dozen of us to join you sounds stupid."

"I thought maybe there would be strength in numbers. Maybe I could finally see her, but when the day came, I couldn't even get myself to drink. That's why I said I would stay behind to watch you. I couldn't get myself to see her, to see the Void. Not again."

I walked over to him. "You condemned my friend to die because of what you told her."

"She's not dead," Walter said, his fingers rapidly clicking on the keyboard. "We'll figure it out."

My phone buzzed with a text, and Gwen's screen lit up, too. It was from Tracy, who was sitting vigil over Trisha at that very moment.

Get here now.

Gwen and I looked at each other, and without another word, we ran out of the room and got in the car.

Chapter 53

Gwen raced through traffic at top speed. I don't know how many red lights we sped through, but I was pretty sure she caused at least two accidents on our way to the hospital. I wasn't complaining, though. Time was of the essence, and after Tracy's first text, she wouldn't respond to anything else, which made me worry even more.

When we got to the hospital, we didn't wait for the nurse to give us our visitor badges. We walked right through to the elevator and took it up to the third floor. Tracy was waiting for us outside of Trisha's room, biting her fingernails.

"What's happening?" I asked, frantic.

"They don't know," Tracy said, quietly. "But it's not good. She's not responding to medication. Her parents are starting to talk about pulling the plug on her."

"They can't do that!" Tears formed in my eyes. "We're so close."

"Well, we're not that close," Gwen said. "But we're closer than we were before, I think."

"I tried to tell them, but they wouldn't listen. How much can I say without sounding like a crazy person? Not much."

"I'm going in," I said. "I'll explain it to them. Everybody already thinks I'm crazy."

Gwen squeezed my hand before I walked into the room. I'm glad she did. I wasn't prepared for the sight of Trisha's withering body. She had withered away to skin and bones. Her cheek bones poked through her skin, and the bags under her eyes expanded to fill nearly half her face. She was pastier than the last time I saw her just a few days before, and now glowed a sweaty white. Trisha barely looked like the person I knew. She was more like a skeleton, or a ghoul.

"Oh my god," I said, placing my hands on my mouth. I didn't want to cry, but I felt the tears coming down my face.

Mrs. And Mr. Burton stood on the other side of Trisha's bed, staring over her like statues, completely in shock. It was likely the same way my mother looked over me, deciding whether to end my life or not.

"Please don't do this," I said.

"Don't judge us." Mrs. Burton looked up at me. "Do you think we want to do this to our little girl? The doctors say there's almost no chance for her to wake up."

"There was no chance for me either, and yet look at me now."

Mr. Burton sucked in his breath. It was uneven, like he was choking on his sadness. "There are only so many miracles to go around, Rebecca. You got yours. We're just not sure there's another one left in this hospital."

"I got two," I said. "I was in two comas, one after the accident and one after the incident in the woods, and I came out of them both. Statistically, that's not likely, but I did it. Your daughter can do it too. You just have to believe in her."

"She's in a better place now," Mrs. Burton said. "Maybe we should let her remain there."

I gritted my teeth. "She is not in a better place. This is a better place. Please, stay strong. Don't pull the plug. I promise you she will come out of this. I swear to you. Please."

I wanted to encourage them, and entreat them to fight with me, but they only looked at me for a moment, then back down at their dying daughter. My hand inched closer to Trisha's. I feared that touching her would connect me with the Void, but I didn't care. I knew where she was, and I knew that in order to keep fighting, she needed to feel me fighting for her.

I placed my hand on Trisha's, waiting for the jolt from the Void, but it never came. After several seconds, I closed my eyes and bowed my head. "Do not take her," I whispered under my breath into the darkness. "Please."

The Void was a ceaseless, horrible thing. I didn't know if it had a soul or could be swayed by pity, but there was a reason it chose me to help it, and if it still wanted my help, then it would need to listen to me.

Chapter 54

I hadn't been home much since I found out that Trisha was in the hospital. I came and went at all hours of the day and night now, and nobody seemed to notice, or if they noticed they didn't say anything to me about it.

"Welcome home," my mother said as I walked in the door. "You've made it home for dinner for once." Mom and Dad were sitting at the table, a pot roast in front of them.

"You set me a place," I said, walking toward them. I hadn't eaten dinner with them for weeks, and yet my mother still put out a place setting for me.

"We always set you a place, dear," Mom said. "I know between basketball and your other obligations, you don't get much time to see us anymore." She paused. "I was hoping after our last conversation you would at least make an effort."

I slid into a chair next to them. I was used to eating my dinner cold in the middle of the night. "I am trying," I replied. "It's just that my friend is very sick, and I've been spending a lot of time with her."

"Is this the Trisha girl who is in a coma?" Mom asked.

I nodded. "Her parents are thinking about pulling the plug on her."

"It's a horrible decision," Mom said. She set a helping of pot roast onto my plate. "I remember your Dad and I sitting up at night trying to figure out what to do with you."

"What made you keep me alive?" I asked.

"We just couldn't do it, kiddo," Dad said. He was pushing food around on his plate absentmindedly. "It was too hard to imagine. It didn't matter if you were in that coma for years, we weren't going to give up on you."

"It must have been so hard, every day, watching me wither away."

Mom reached out and grabbed Dad's hand. "It was so hard. They never tell you how hard it's going to be as a parent. It's hard decision after hard decision every single day."

I smiled at them. "Thank you for not giving up on me."

"Well, we couldn't do it." Dad took a bite of food. "I don't know if that made us stupid or brave, but it worked out."

I looked at both of them, feeling the tears form in my eyes. "I'm not just talking about the coma. I'm talking about everything. This whole year, you've always been there, in your way."

"We'd do anything for you, kiddo," Dad said. He reached out and rubbed my arm.

"Do you think I might be able to see that psychologist again? I always felt better after seeing her."

"Of course," Dad said. "Make an appointment and I'll take you."

I forgot how nice it was to eat a quiet dinner with my family. Being there with both of my parents, in my house, where I felt safe, was everything. I felt a pang, thinking of Mary.

"Have you been sleeping?" Mom asked, pointing to the bags under my eyes. "You look horrible."

I shook my head. "It's been a lot, Mom."

She touched my hand. "It will get better. I promise you that."

"When?"

"Eventually." She smiled at me, but her eyes were sad.

After dinner I could barely keep my eyes open. I stumbled into my room, and barely got to my bed before collapsing on top of it. I didn't want to close my eyes, knowing what I'd see, but my body wouldn't let me move any more. I needed to sleep.

My eyes closed and immediately, the Void flashed before me. I saw Trisha there, locked in the arms of the fiery Void, but she wasn't alone. Next to her, glowing blue like Thomas, was the haunting visage of my sister. She looked as beautiful in death as she did in life.

They were bound together, screaming in agony. Their agonizing pain rang through my ears. The message was clear: I was running out of time. If I didn't hurry, those whom I loved would be tortured mercilessly until the end of eternity.

I wanted to hurry. I desperately wanted to know the correct way forward, but I was grasping at straws.

Chapter 55

"Thank you for bringing me here," I said to my mother. We stood in front of my sister's grave. I hadn't been there since the funeral. I brought flowers, and Mom brought her a Saint Christopher medal, the patron saint of travelers. Giant clouds loomed over our heads as we stared at the headstone.

"It's going to rain soon," Mom said absently.

"I miss her," I said. "I miss her so much."

"I miss her, too." Mom placed a gentle hand on my shoulder. "We will always miss her."

"You said you heard the Void, too."

"I did. All through my childhood. It beckoned me to join it. It was merciless."

"How did you get over it?" I asked.

She smiled. "I became friends with the darkness eventually. The world is a cold place, and it will beat you if you let it. The Void promised me warmth, and it was inviting, but that is not the truth of the world. The world is cold, so bitterly cold. When I learned that, and embraced it, the cold didn't seem so frightening."

"It's frightening to me."

Mom smiled at me. "We all deal with the cold, every one of us, in our own way, and yet, humanity continues to soldier on through it all. Every person you pass is fighting a demon, my love. If you beat the Void, there will be another obstacle waiting for you. As they say, every level, another devil. All we can do is keep jumping into the fray."

"That is…surprisingly comforting."

"The more I understood that everybody somehow fights the cold, every day, the more reason I had to fight my own battles. I mean, if they could do it, so could I. I started living for that reason, and then I found another reason, and another, and another. Eventually, I had you, and that was my reason."

I placed my hand on Mom's. "Thank you."

"No, Becca. Thank you."

Chapter 56

Paintings of the Void hung all around Doctor Thatcher's office. They were on every wall in her waiting room, and her therapy room. I didn't know if it was elegant or macabre to hang a symbol of death in one's office.

For myself, I found them both comforting and terrifying. It reminded me that I was not alone in my struggle. We were all battling the Void together. Some of us won, and others of us, like my sister, lost. It was a battle waged across the world, and it was hard for me not to take some solace in that. I was not alone.

"These paintings," my father said. "They are a bit creepy, aren't they?"

I nodded. "They sure are. This is what I see when I close my eyes, so I am very comfortable with them, in an odd way."

"This is that Void thingy you have been talking about, right?"

"Well, they are artist's interpretations, so they are far less creepy than what I see when I close my eyes, but yes, basically. Welcome to my nightmare."

Doctor Thatcher stuck her head out of her office and beckoned me inside. "Come in, Rebecca. It's your turn."

I passed a gaunt man in a trench coat too thick for his body, as if he'd shrunk ten sizes since buying it. He was coming out of her office. As we passed each other, I saw the horror staring back at me from behind his eyes. Even though I had never met him before, I felt his pain.

"How are you feeling today, Rebecca?"

I sat down across from her. "Not good, I'm afraid, and I'm sorry to say that I did not come for therapy today, Doctor."

"Then what are you here for?" she asked. "I'm afraid I'm not set up for social calls."

"I came because I have a question for you, and I'm hoping you can answer it without thinking me too odd."

"I don't think any of my patients are odd, Rebecca, just in pain and needing guidance."

"Good, because I came to become better informed, and I do need your guidance, if you will give it to me."

"I will help in any way I can."

"I'm going to speak frankly to you, as I believe you need to hear the truth." I took a breath. "The Void is a malevolent being which calls out to humanity like a giant fly catcher, trying to woo us into its clutches, where it can consume us forever."

"That is a wild theory, Rebecca. What makes you say that?"

"I say it because it is the truth. I have ventured into the maw of the Void, and I have seen its true colors. Now, I need to return something to it, something that was taken, or it will consume my friend's soul, and she will never wake up."

"Yes, I heard about your friend Trisha. That is such a sad story. I know you want to help her." She shifted in her seat. "Concocting a story like this is not uncommon for somebody in your situation. We want to feel like we are in control, but the truth is, some things just happen in this world for no rhyme or reason, and there is nothing we can do about it."

I nodded. "I know that, but I can do something about this. Trisha journeyed to the Void and took something. I need to give it back if I'm going to save her."

Doctor Thatcher leaned forward. "All right, I'll bite. What did she bring back?"

"She brought back her boyfriend's soul, and now the Void wants it back."

"Her boyfriend? She brought him back…to Earth."

"Well, I don't know exactly what happened, but something that she did unleashed his spirit, and he came back to Earth. Now, the Void wants him back, and I need to know if you've come across any research about bringing the dead back to the Void."

Doctor Thatcher sat back in her chair. "Are you trying to go back? Because I believe that if you are trying to commit suicide again—"

"I'm not trying to kill myself. I'm just asking a question. Have you ever heard of anything like that, where people need to bargain with the Void, or bring something to it from our world?"

"I could have you committed for this kind of thing, but I think you need something else, something to show where this path will lead you."

"Anything."

Doctor Thatcher tapped her pen a few times, as if thinking. "I had a client once. He was not unlike you, until he had a psychotic break. He told me all sorts of wild stories about bringing his dead daughter back from the Void. You might say he was the man that piqued my interest in this work."

"Who is he?"

"Did you know, I've lived here my entire life, right in this town? It's where I started my practice. It's where I took in my first clients. It's where I took him in and cared for him, before he was sent away."

"His name, Doctor. What was his name?"

"You should look into the newspaper clippings for December thirteenth, in 2001. I was a witness at the trial to commit him. Doctor Ursula Thatcher. I'm afraid that's all I can give you."

I sighed. "It's enough, I hope."

"I beg you, do not go down this road. It only leads to madness."

I stood up. "I have to do everything I can to help my friend."

Chapter 57

The minute I got home from Doctor Thatcher's office I used my computer to look up court cases from December of 2001. Unfortunately, neither the newspaper or the court had online documents dating back that far, which meant I would need to go to the library. I called up Gwen and she picked me up at my house.

"Do you even know how to use one of these things?" Gwen asked as we walked back to the microfilm readers with a box of film.

"Yeah, I had to do a paper last year on the nineties, and one of my main sources wasn't online. The librarians taught me how to do it."

Microfilm readers were basically big, bulky projectors that magnified film. You spooled the film canister through the television-like device, and then used a hand crank to spin it forward. Before the internet, research was much harder.

As I cranked the film through the projector, the headlines for the *Daily Bugle* spun back through newspapers from 2001. Even two months after the incident, 9/11 still occupied the front headlines of the newspapers, even in our little corner of the world.

"Wait," Gwen said, placing her hand on mine. As she did, a spark of electricity jolted through me, and I jumped. "Sorry," she said, drawing her hand back.

"It's okay."

"Look at that," she said, pointing to an article from December thirteenth.

Local Man Found Guilty of 1ˢᵗ Degree Murder

Local man, Robert Samson, was found
guilty of first-degree murder for the
death of his brother Jonathan Samson.
Doctor Ursula Thatcher was
instrumental in getting the murderer
declared criminally insane and sentenced
to live out the remainder of his days at
Stoneybrooke Hospital.

"This must be it!" I said, jumping up and down in my chair.

"Hang on," Gwen said. "Read the second paragraph."

When asked why he committed the
murder, Mister Samson said that he
needed to "return his daughter to the
Void" and his brother "offered to deliver
her."

"Whoa," Gwen said. "According to this, we might have to kill somebody else in order to return Thomas to the Void? How is that fair?"

"I don't know. And the only way we're going to figure it out is by talking to this guy." I peered at the screen. "Robert Samson."

"Oh, good," she said. "That makes total sense. Let's go take advice from a crazy person."

"Yes. Let's."

Chapter 58

Stoneybrooke Hospital was a two-hour drive, which meant that we needed to get up early in the morning if Gwen and I wanted to drive there and back in a single day. I brought the coffee and Gwen brought the car. We listened to angry girl rock all the way up, from Joan Jett to the Veronicas to Haim.

Gwen never liked to stay on any one band for too long, which made my Spotify playlist perfect. I had been working on it since I first found The Void Calls Us Home and figured the perfect time to play it was during a long road trip.

"Why did you decide to start a band with Trisha?" I asked. "You two seem so different."

"She was cool, I guess. And damaged, like me, which I liked. Plus, have you heard her sing? I mean, of course you heard her sing. That girl was made to be a star."

"Baggage and all," I added.

She chuckled. "Got that right. The baggage might've made her even more of a star, honestly."

The longer I hung out with Gwen, the more I liked her. I'd had a fleeting infatuation with Trisha, but she always wanted things her way. Gwen treated me like an equal, a person with my own hopes and dreams. She never pushed me to be like her. She wanted me to be like me.

"Remember what you said the first time we met?" I asked.

"Of course. I said I thought you were cute, and I wanted to call you."

"That was so corny and lame."

Gwen shrugged. "You still gave me your number."

"I was just so stunned that somebody could be so cheesy."

"And yet, look at us now."

I smiled, cocking my head toward her. "Yeah, look at us now."

When we finally got up to the hospital it was half past ten, and visiting hours were in full swing. Dozens of cars lined the parking lot, and families funneled out of their cars into the facility.

"There's not a lot of people who come to see old Robbie," the receptionist said when we reached the front desk. "He scares most people."

I shot a smile at her. "Well, I'm very anxious to meet him. My mother told me all about cousin Robbie from back east, and once I heard his tragic story I just had to come visit."

Tracy had concocted a long and elaborate back story, but I didn't need it. It turned out that anybody could see Robbie if they just asked. We could have said we were organ harvesters and they would have let us see him.

We followed the nurse through the dark hallways and into a wide, grassy area behind the hospital. It was a lovely day and families were visiting with each other throughout the grounds. Between them all, sitting on a metal bench, staring off into space, was a gray-haired man with a light blue sweater on, who had a look of pain in his eyes.

"That's Robbie," she said. "You be nice. He hasn't had a visitor in a while."

We thanked her and walked down the stairs onto the grass. "Mister Samson?" I asked as we neared him.

"Who's asking?" he replied without looking up.

"My name is Rebecca," I said, pointing to myself. "This is Gwen. We're here to ask you a few questions."

"Are you reporters?" he said. "Reporters like to ask questions. Never get it right, though."

I shook my head. "No, I'm not a reporter. I'm a high school student, and my friend is in trouble. I think you can help her."

"Why me?" he asked.

"Because she's been captured by the Void."

His eyes went wide, and his jaw clenched. "How long?"

"A while now," Gwen said. "Couple of weeks."

"Horrible," Robbie said. "The Void is a horrible being."

"What is it?" I asked. "Do you know?"

"Of course I know. The Void is one of a thousand creatures that roam the night. They might be gods. I don't know, but they are more powerful and horrible than you can imagine. They feed on humanity, and the Void, Z'li'thol, is no different."

"Z'li'thol," I whispered.

"The name of the Void in the mother tongue," Robbie asked, his voice cracking. "What does it want?"

"He wants a soul that was taken from him to be returned. I thought you might know how to give it back."

"It is very hard," Robbie said. "Especially hard to return something that was taken. You are meant to walk alone in the darkness. That is how Z'li'thol comes for you, when you are alone. It feeds on your negative thoughts, and uses them against you to drive you mad, until you have no choice but to join him."

"Last time I willingly journeyed to the Void, I was supposed to travel with my friend, but when I woke up in the black ether, I was alone."

"That is how it's meant to be. That is how the Void likes it."

I considered this for a moment. "But it doesn't have to be that way?"

Robbie shook his head. "No. You can bind a soul to you, but the costs are great."

"Please, tell me how to do it."

Tears streamed down Robbie's face. "I only wanted to see my daughter again. She was taken from me too soon. After her death, I studied. I studied everything, and in studying I learned you could retrieve a soul from the Void."

"But they don't come back the same," I said, quietly.

"No, they don't, but I didn't know that then. In my studies, I learned how to visit the Void, and then I did." Robbie kept on. "I wanted my daughter back, and so I took her. I took her from the mouth of that mad fool creature, but something wasn't right when we got back home. Jenny wasn't right. She wasn't right. She couldn't—she didn't—she didn't speak. She couldn't move. All she did was stare off into space. She wasn't my Jenny, and she never would be. I knew I had to give her back to the Void."

"How did you do it? How did you return her to the Void? Souls aren't supposed to travel together."

"First, I bound my soul to hers through a blood ritual," Robbie said, choking on his tears.

"How did you bind her soul to yours?" Gwen asked.

"With my brother's blood. His life was what was required in order to bind my daughter's soul with mine, so we could make the journey together into the great beyond. My brother agreed willingly. He had seen how horribly Jenny suffered. For my daughter's life, he gave his as a sacrifice. He slit his own throat as I watched. It was horrible."

"So, you're not a murderer?"

"No, I'm worse. I was complicit. I let him do it. I let him sacrifice himself to return my daughter to the Void."

"And did it work?" Gwen asked.

He nodded sadly. "It worked for our purposes, but they were horrible purposes. The blood ritual bound my daughter's soul to mine, and I brought her back to the Void. I watched her enter the black goop and never got to say goodbye. The Void took her willingly, and it took my brother as a sacrifice as well."

"How did you perform the ritual?" I asked. "We need specifics."

His eyes narrowed. "Why?"

Gwen and I exchanged a long look. Finally, she answered, "We need to return a soul to the Void."

"No!" Robbie shouted. "I won't let you do it again. NURSE!" He stood up and started back across the grass. "Nurse! I think it's time for my meds!"

"Another dead end," I said. "We're running out of time."

"At least we know one part of it," she said. "But I don't know who you're going to sacrifice to give Thomas back."

I didn't either. I wasn't about to kill somebody for the Void, or for Trisha. There had to be another way I wasn't seeing, but that's the problem with walking in the dark. You have no idea how close you are to an exit.

Chapter 59

"I'm not going to kill anyone," I said as we drove back from the hospital.

"Nobody's killing anybody," Gwen agreed.

"What are we going to do then? Robbie literally just said he had to kill somebody in order to return his daughter to the Void."

"Sure," Gwen said. "But he's just one person. And he was committed to an insane asylum."

"That doesn't make him crazy. He just happened to succeed at returning somebody to the Void," I said. "Which is something we need to do and as far as I know, he's the only person who's done it."

"There have to be others who've done it. Let's just keep digging."

We drove right to Walter's house. His house still smelt like cheese and Thomas's ghost still hovered in the corner, sullen and mute. Nothing had changed, and my attitude was much less optimistic.

"How did it go?" Walter asked.

"Horrible," I replied. "Apparently, we have to kill somebody in order to return Thomas to the Void."

"Is that what Robbie said?" Walter asked.

"Yup," Gwen replied.

"I assume he's talking about soul binding, then?"

"That's right."

"In that case, I think he's wrong," Walter said with a smirk. "Soul binding often requires a human sacrifice, but I might have found another way." He handed us two stacks of papers from off his desk. "Open to page fifteen."

I placated him and opened to the page. The heading read, *"The Binding Ritual of Ug'la'zha."*

"What is this?" I asked.

"Okay, so remember the last time you went into the Void you were holding Trisha's hand, and when you woke up, she wasn't there?"

"Yes," I replied.

"Well, that's because every soul is supposed to enter the eternal darkness alone. However, this spell binds one soul to another soul, allowing them to journey together through the cosmic darkness together."

"So, if we perform this ritual, then I drink that horrible concoction you made, I should wake up with Thomas in the Void?"

"Yes, but there is one problem," he said. "It tells us how to bind a soul to you, but I haven't found a way to tear it apart."

"So, if I don't figure that part out then I could be dragged into the Void with Thomas when I return him?"

He nodded. "It looks that way."

My phone rang. It was Tracy texting from the hospital.

They are going to do it. Get here now if you want to say goodbye.

"I have to go," I said, rushing toward the door. "Can you figure out how to set this up alone?"

Walter nodded. "I think so. It will take a couple hours."

"We might not have a couple hours," I said. "Gwen, we need to go, now."

Chapter 60

Gwen and I rushed to the hospital, though I worried it would not be fast enough. I thought my presence would have swayed them to keep Trisha alive for longer. Not that I was a great orator, but I had beaten the odds twice which proved it was possible for anybody. I was not particularly lucky. I was just a survivor, and Trisha was a survivor too. She would make it through this.

By the time we got into Trisha's room, the doctor had gathered Mr. and Mrs. Burton around to say goodbye. Everybody in the room was crying, except for the doctor, who dealt with death on a regular basis. Even Tracy was crying, and she didn't like Trisha.

"Please don't do this," I said, walking into the room.

"Yeah, Mr. and Mrs. Burton," Gwen added. "Trisha could still come back."

"The odds against that are astronomical," the doctor said. "This is the best choice for her, and for us. We have to move on now."

"No, you don't! It's not over!" I shouted. "You're going to kill her."

"She's already dead!" Mrs. Burton said through gritted teeth. "You just haven't admitted it to yourself yet."

"I'll never admit it," I said, tears streaming down my face. "We're so close. Please, just give us one more day."

"Silly girl," Mr. Burton said. "Nothing you can do will help her. She's on her own."

I took another step forward. "How long will it take? How long will it take for her to die?"

The doctor turned to me. "Once we remove the tubes, she could be alive for minutes or hours. It depends on how strong of a fighter she is."

"She's strong," I said. "She'll fight. Come on, Gwen. We've got to work fast. Tracy—"

"I know," Tracy said. "Stay here and tell you if anything changes."

"No," I said, walking over to her. "Try to keep her alive. Please. For as long as you can."

"How am I supposed to do that?"

I shrugged. "Stall them. Anything. Trisha's not dying tonight. Not if we have anything to say about it."

"What if you don't?" Tracy asked, choking back her tears.

"We will," I said. "Please believe that."

It took us fifteen minutes to get back to Walter's house. When we entered, he had cleared out his living room and carved a pentagram into the floor. Above the pentagram, Thomas's ghost hovered, and on every corner of the pentagram a candle burned.

"Is it ready?" I asked, out of breath.

"Almost," he said. "If I've done this right. First, we do the binding, then you drink the juice."

"We don't have that kind of time. We'll have to do them together."

"That could kill you," he replied.

"So could life. Where is the juice?"

Walter pointed to a plastic Star Trek cup on the table. I picked it up and downed it in one gulp. "What now?"

"Middle of the circle," he said, reaching back for a stack of papers and handing it to Gwen. "Gwen, you get across from me and get ready to chant. Got it?"

"Got it," she said. "You know, I spent so much time trying to convince Trisha this was stupid, I never thought I would be doing one of these rituals."

"Life is funny," I said, laying in the middle of the circle. My eyes were already getting droopy. "I'm glad you're here."

Gwen squeezed my hand. "Me too."

"Don't forget," Walter said. "If you don't find a way to unbind the enchantment, you'll be stuck, bound to Thomas forever."

"Don't remind me," I said. Above me, Thomas's ghost hovered, covering my field of vision.

"All right," Walter said. "Begin."

Ug'la'zha, c' uln thee. ah'ehye cahff orr'ee ehye. f' uaaah ehye. Ug'la'zha, c' uln thee. ah'ehye cahff orr'ee ehye. f' uaaah ehye. Ug'la'zha, c' uln thee. ah'ehye cahff orr'ee ehye. f' uaaah ehye.

I felt a twinge of pain in my finger tips that rose up my body, through my wrists, and into my forearms, my shoulders, and eventually my chest. The same sting rose from my feet to my thighs and to my stomach. The twinge of pain became a throb, which in turn became a searing light, which worked its way from my bones out to my skin, until I was convulsing with pain.

Ug'la'zha, c' uln thee. ah'ehye cahff orr'ee ehye. f' uaaah ehye. Ug'la'zha, c' uln thee. ah'ehye cahff orr'ee ehye. f' uaaah ehye. Ug'la'zha, c' uln thee. ah'ehye cahff orr'ee ehye. f' uaaah ehye.

"STOP!" I shouted, but they wouldn't stop.

Ug'la'zha, c' uln thee. ah'ehye cahff orr'ee ehye. f' uaaah ehye. Ug'la'zha, c' uln thee. ah'ehye cahff orr'ee ehye. f' uaaah ehye. Ug'la'zha, c' uln thee. ah'ehye cahff orr'ee ehye. f' uaaah ehye.

My eyes opened. The blue aura surrounding Thomas glowed brightly, pulsating along with my pain, and then, in an instant, his soul collapsed into a ball like a white dwarf star, and fell into my chest. The pain dissipated, like a cooling bath.

I opened my eyes to look out, but everything was blurry. My head was spinning. I collapsed back onto the ground. I fell into the darkness and it expanded around me to fill every corner of my vision.

Chapter 61

When my eyes popped open, I was hovering, suspended in the ether, just like I had in my previous journeys into the Void. However, instead of nothing but black surrounding me, I was joined by a blue aura. I looked over to see Thomas, shackled to me like a prisoner, floating, hollow and sad.

"I'm sorry about this," I said, looking at him. "I know it must be terrible to live in the Void." He nodded, or at least I thought it was a nod. "And I know I never asked you what you wanted, but Trisha is in trouble, and it's my job to save her. Do you want to save her?"

Thomas nodded again. He turned toward the darkness, and in it, I saw a pinprick of light.

"Let's go," I said.

I swam forward and as I did the pinprick grew and grew. "I don't suppose you have any idea how to unbind us, do you?"

Thomas shook his head. I didn't expect him to have an answer, but I had to ask. I was willing to give myself to the Void if it meant I could save my friend, but if I didn't have to do that…it would be preferable.

"I'll figure something out."

The deep voice of the Void quaked in the distance. "You have returned."

"I have," I said.

"Only too soon. I can only keep poor Trisha alive for so much longer. Even now her parents work to send her to me forever."

The great chasm of the Void widened. "Give him to me," the Void rumbled. "Make me whole again. Give back the soul you have taken from me."

"Release Trisha like you promised."

"This is not a game, child. You have no power here."

I threw my shoulders back and lifted my chin. I would not be intimidated. "Perhaps not, but I have what you seek. If you want it, release her, and I will release him."

The Void grumbled. "Very well."

The fiery arms of the flaming souls around the edge of the Void let go of Trisha and she floated off into space toward me. Her soul was thin and weak. She could barely lift her head to look at me when I grabbed her.

"Thank you," I said, looking down at Trisha's hollow face.

"I have lived up to my end of the bargain," the Void shouted. "Now it is your turn."

A great wind blew from the base of the Void, pulling Thomas toward it. I grabbed onto Trisha to steady myself, but I couldn't hold on to her without pulling all three of us back toward the Void. I was bound to Thomas, and so the Void sucked me toward its mouth as well, but Trisha could still live free.

"Let me go!"

I scratched at the air as I fell toward the event horizon of the Void's black maw. A great bolt of blue light shot out from the black ooze. It flew toward me at incredible speed and sliced through my arm.

I screamed in pain and watched the blue light as it turned around toward me. It stopped for a moment and I barely made out Mary's face in the blur of light.

"Mary!" I shouted.

She didn't respond, except to give a slight smile. Then, she flew forward again, faster than before, toward me. As she passed between me and the Void, she exploded in a firework of blue light. The explosion blew me free from Thomas and sent him flying toward the mouth of the great Void.

Meanwhile, the energy blast knocked me back toward Trisha, and clear from the Void. My sister rematerialized in its mouth as it collapsed upon itself. She waved at me, reaching with her arms, and fell back into the Void.

"Mary!" I shouted, but it was too late to save her. The Void had taken her with it. I couldn't save her, but I could still help Trisha. I grabbed her and pulled her away from the light.

"Trisha," I said. "Trisha, honey. Come on, get up."

"Wha...?" she replied, slowly.

"You need to get up now, Trisha. You need to do it now. Your parents, they don't think you will ever wake up. Please, Trisha. Please. Wake up."

Trisha's eyes opened and she looked at me. Then, a moment later, she vanished. She was gone. I didn't know where she went, but I hoped whatever I said knocked something loose in her so she could return from the darkness.

I closed my eyes and took a deep breath. It was time to go back. It was time to go home. I opened my eyes and looked out into the Void one last time, but I could no longer see it in the darkness.

Chapter 62

"Trisha!" I shouted.

I pushed myself up from the floor in Walter's house, taking huge gulps of air.

"Oh, thank god you're alive," Gwen said, throwing herself back against the couch. "I thought for sure we killed you."

"We have to go," I said.

"You keep saying that," Gwen said. "I'm not a chauffeur."

"C'mon, hurry! We have to see if she's awake."

"You should check your phone," Gwen said, still sitting on the couch. She held up her phone. On it was a text from Tracy with a picture of Trisha smiling.

"It worked," Walter said, staring at the ceiling in relief. "Thank god it worked."

Gwen and I piled into her station wagon and drove to the hospital. Tracy threw her arms around me when she saw me and led me into the room.

"It's a miracle," Mrs. Burton said.

Trisha and I looked at each other. We knew it wasn't a miracle. We knew exactly what happened. She beckoned me over and wrapped her arms around mine.

"When I'm feeling better," Trisha said, squeezing me tightly, "I demand you tell me everything that happened after you woke up."

"Gladly," I said. "I'm glad you're alive, still."

"Thanks to you," she said, kissing me on the cheek.

Weeks ago, it would have blown my mind to get a kiss from Trisha, but things had changed since then. Her kiss did nothing but make my eyes shoot immediately to Gwen, who had been there for me this whole time.

Gwen walked out of the room as the rest of the family celebrated, and I unwrapped from Trisha. "I'll be right back."

"Okay," she said, wearily.

I ran out into the hall to see Gwen leaning up against the wall. "Why do you look so sad? This is a happy day."

"I'm happy," Gwen said. "Don't I look happy?"

I shook my head. "No, you look like death warmed over."

"You would know," she said with a sigh. "I guess everything goes back to normal now."

"Hey," I said, grabbing her hands. "What is normal, anyway?"

She squeezed my hand tightly. "True."

It took three more days for Trisha to get out of the hospital, and then another week for her to start school again. When she did, I was surprised at how normal everything was in a short time. I no longer slept with fear, and neither did Trisha. I don't know what my sister did to the Void, but it left us alone from then on. Neither my mother nor I ever heard from it again.

We won regionals in basketball but lost in the state finals. I was very little help in that respect. I was a very good water wench, though. Next year I planned to be back, and in better shape. Tracy promised to help me with my game over the summer, but I wasn't too upset about it. I had already moved on to track season and was building my endurance back up. Sometimes, Gwen even ran with me, when she didn't have a gig.

Mom and I started talking more, and we finally began speaking the same language. Every Thursday we brought a bouquet of flowers to my sister's grave. I knew she was out there, somewhere, and she had saved my life more than once. One day, maybe I'll see her again, but no time soon.

Death will always follow me, for as long as I live. I don't think I will ever shake the dark feelings bubbling deep inside me, but now, I just want to live.

Author Notes

Writing this book was my reward for writing fifteen books in 2018. I enjoy writing contemporary YA books about death, grief, and loss. That was the theme for *My Father Didn't Kill Himself* and *Sorry for Existing,* but since then I had focused my writing on more fantasy and sci-fi work, taking places in magical and enchanted realms.

This book was a return to form for me, and the first love of my writing life. This wasn't a big story, but it was an important one to me. I often see the Void in my own life and have learned to deal with it much like Rebecca's mother learned to deal with her own darkness.

The first draft of this book was a nightmare. I only had a rough outline before I started, and it wasn't until I was more than 80 percent done with the first draft that I had a theme in mind, and then I had to seed that through the book and weave it back through in the subsequent drafts.

It started to come together during the second draft the more I thought about cosmic horror, and specifically Lovecraft. I am a huge fan of Lovecraft's universe, and specifically the relationship between his characters and the gods around them. There has always been a depth to Lovecraft's stories that transcends a lot of other writers, because he dealt with the human condition, and our place as an insignificant part of the cosmos. I relate to that on a deep, visceral level.

I edited an anthology called *Cthulhu is Hard to Spell* in 2018, so I have a deep affinity for Lovecraft. In fact, the incantations you read on these pages are R'lyehian, which I pulled straight from the R'lyehian-English translator online. Still, I wouldn't call this a horror book, per se, though it has many cosmic horror elements.

Once I figured out the Lovecraftian part of the story, the rest of it made sense. I found my voice and my rhythm, and the themes started to resonate with me. I knew I wanted to write another story about death and grief, but I originally thought it was going to be about Rebecca dealing with her own attempted suicide. I didn't realize until much later that she was really dealing with her sister's suicide instead.

It took longer to figure that part out than in any book I've ever written, or possibly it just felt like that because I didn't spend as much time writing an outline as I normally do in my other books.

I can't believe I didn't used to write outlines. This book was SO tough because I tried to discover the theme and plot throughout. Working without an outline used to be my preferred strategy even. However, doing so in this book was very difficult.

It took most of the first draft, but I figured it out, and I think it turned out okay. I hope you agree. I am a huge fan of books that deal with death, grief, loss, and junk, and if you are too then I hope you got a ton out of this book.

I'm not sure though, because I'm not the reader. I just wrote the thing. If you want to find more books about death, grief, loss, and junk, head over to my website and sign up for my mailing list at:

*

If you liked this book, make sure to check out *Anna and the Dark Place*, a dark fantasy about a girl whose best friend comes back from the dead to help her mend a tear in the divide between the living and the dead. Here's a preview of the book.

Anna and the Dark Place

By:

Russell Nohelty

Edited by:

Leah Lederman

Proofread by:

Katrina Roets

Cover by:

Paramita Bhattacharjee

Chapter 1

Funerals suck.

That wasn't some great revelation or anything, but just because it wasn't profound didn't make it any less true. I wasn't trying to be Shakespeare. Every word out of my mouth or thought in my head didn't need to be some pithy observation meant to entertain a billion people for a thousand years.

In my short sixteen years of life, I'd been to four funerals, though, so I knew something about the subject: all of them sucked, hard. I wasn't a mob hitman. Why had I been to so many funerals at such a tender age? Some people chalked it up to bad luck, but I had the sneaking suspicion I was cursed.

The first funeral I attended was for my nana. She was old, and I was three. I couldn't remember that one very well because…well, I was three. Who remembers anything from when they were three? Nobody, that's who.

Next was my Aunt Pauline. She smoked a pack of cigarettes a day until the day she died. I wasn't surprised she died young, but I was surprised she could afford the habit even after they raised the price to over seven dollars a pack. I guess it was lucky that she retired rich with the right stock options. Or maybe it wasn't lucky, since those cigarettes killed her.

The third funeral was my father's, and it sucked super hard. Kids are supposed to outlive their parents, but that didn't make it suck any less. Parents were supposed to die after they'd gotten older, like when they were ninety, not when they were forty-five.

Although, maybe I need to shut my mouth, because it's better to outlive your parent than to have your parent outlive you.

Katie was my best friend, and the owner of the body that was being lowered into the ground in front of me. We had known each other all of our lives. Our parents brought us home from the hospital within a month of each other, and our fathers left us at the same time, both through the same helicopter accident in Kabul which killed their whole unit.

Crap. I had been to five funerals. I forgot that Katie's father had a funeral the day after my father's, so they blended together.

Katie and I grew up across the street from each other, and our families did everything together, from having barbecues, to watching the Super Bowl, to going on vacations together. After our fathers died, Katie and Joanne became even closer to us. We didn't have much family left. My father was an only child, and my mother only had Pauline. Once they were gone, and Nana too, our family became just my mother, me, Katie, and Joanne.

I hated death with a real passion, too. It wasn't fair. All the other kids had brothers, sisters, cousins, aunts, uncles, fathers, grandparents…they had a family. They had friends. They had support.

Death took all of that away from me. Every person I grew close to faded out of my life. After my father died, I stopped letting people in. I walled myself off from the outside world. I figured if everybody was going to die, and it hurt so bad every time they did, at least I could be hurt by as few people as possible.

I didn't join any clubs, or play any sports, or go to any parties. All I did was come home after school and hang out with Katie, and whatever friends she bothered to bring around me. She never had the same fears I did, despite death taking her father away just like it had mine.

She was the opposite of me. After her father's death, Katie decided to go out into the world and meet new people. She signed up for all the clubs and never met a person she didn't like. She lived more in her few years on this planet than most people, and certainly had more of a life than I ever did.

Joanne stood from her seat next to mine in the cemetery and walked up to the podium beside Katie's grave. Her hair was once blonde and vibrant, but she long ago let it return to its natural brown, which matched her eyes. Her skin was white and pale, and her eyes were red from crying.

"Thank you for coming," Joanna said, as her daughter was lowered into the grave in front of her. "I know it's not normal to give the eulogy at the cemetery instead of a church, but my Katie wasn't normal, either."

Katie had planned her own funeral, which was how I learned that the difference between a cemetery and a graveyard is that a graveyard is connected to a church and a cemetery isn't connected to anything. Katie hated churches, and she refused to be buried in a graveyard. She wanted her funeral to take place outdoors, not in some stuffy funeral parlor.

Joanne wiped the tears from her eyes. "Katie told me the day she was diagnosed that she was going to die, but that didn't stop her from fighting anyway."

It was true. I was there. Specifically, what she said was, "Mom, I don't think I'm going to beat this cancer, but I'm not going down without a fight." That was the kind of person Katie was, practical but headstrong. She ended up being right too, about her death at least, which I hated her for just a little bit, which made me love her just 9,999,999 percent more than anybody else.

"She wasn't scared of death," Joanne continued, choking on her tears. "Even in the last days of her life, she saw it as another step in the journey. She didn't know where she was going to go, but she knew it would be a better place."

That part was a lie, but at least it was only a lie of omission. She said it wouldn't be any worse of a place, or at least that's what she told me. She could have said something different to her mother. Then, she only would have been lying to one of us, but Katie always believed that lies were okay as long as they came from a place of kindness.

"I know she's in a better place." Joanne paused, swallowing her tears. "And one day we will be together again in the next life. Until then, Katie would have wanted me to live. She would have wanted us all to live; to embrace life, and to cherish every day as if it were our last."

That did sound like her. Hopelessly optimistic even in the end, even when she had no reason to be optimistic. "Cheer up," she would tell me whenever I visited her in the hospital during her chemo treatments. "I'm the one dying."

She was wrong, of course. We were all the ones dying. She was just dying sooner than the rest of us. One day we would all be dead. What would happen to me then? Would I really be reunited with Katie, or would I just rot in the ground?

Joanne grabbed a rose from the foldout table next to her. There were over a hundred roses piled there. I looked around and there were only a few dozen people in attendance, but that was Katie, always hopelessly optimistic, even about how many people would attend her funeral.

I helped Katie plan her funeral, once the tumors in her bones became inoperable. She wanted me to put a clown nose on her, and make sure everybody honked it when they passed. It was the only thing Joanne refused to do for her after she died. It was a shame, because that was a perfectly Katie moment, laughing at death and making everybody around her feel slightly less uncomfortable.

After a moment of silent contemplation, Joanne turned to us again. "Now, please step forward and send my daughter into the afterlife with a rose."

I walked forward with my mother and picked up three roses, then headed slowly toward the grave where the coffin was already lowered.

"I wish we had more time together," I whispered. I threw the roses into the hole in the ground which held my best friend's body. "Goodbye."

Chapter 2

Katie had hundreds of friends before she was diagnosed with leukemia. They came to sleepovers at her house and cheered her on during soccer games. Everybody said they loved her. People loved Katie…but then she became sick. Once she got sick, the number of friends she had whittled down until there was just me again.

It was the best part of Katie being sick, honestly. I finally got to hang out with her without a gaggle of other friends around. Most of middle school saw me watching from the sidelines as Katie did one amazing thing after another, leaving me behind little by little. She kept me around once she became popular, but it was never the same as when we were younger.

Don't get me wrong. I absolutely hated that Katie had cancer, but that didn't mean it was without its benefits. Most things, no matter how horrible, had tangential benefits. Hell, they say Hitler kept the trains running on time, but that doesn't mean anybody wanted another Holocaust.

Everybody abandoned Katie once the cancer got hard, and she stopped being peppy all the time, which meant she needed a friend. A real friend. Somebody who wouldn't complain when she couldn't go out on Friday night. One that held her hair when she threw up and who told her she looked good when all that hair came out during the horrible days after chemo when all she wanted to do was cry and sleep.

I was glad that person was me. We would stay up late at night, read books together, and talk about life and the universe, just like when we were kids. I never begrudged Katie her accolades or friendships. I really, seriously wanted what was best for her. I never wanted her to be sick and hoped against hope that she was wrong about dying. It turned out everything she said would happen, did happen.

I ended up in Katie's room an hour after the funeral, looking out at my pale, purple house across the street. It sorely needed a paint job. Every night, Katie and I would say goodnight to each other through our windows, and every morning I would rush to the window to make sure she was still alive.

When I woke up on the day she died, her mother was in her room, crying. I watched her scream and collapse on her daughter's lifeless corpse. I knew what had happened, but that didn't stop me from running across the street and pushing open the front door that Joanne never locked.

Katie didn't look dead when I saw her the morning after she died. She was pale, but she had been paling for months, and she was so skinny in the final months of her life that I could see her bones through her sagging skin. Her blonde hair had long ago fallen out, and her dark blue eyes were closed as if she were sleeping.

She died in her sleep, and I wasn't there to comfort her. Nobody was there for her in those final moments.

I was likely the last person to see her alive. Her mother had kissed her goodnight and tucked her in before we waved to each other that night. Had I known it would be the last time I saw her, I would have said more; I would have told her how I really felt about her, but I had no clue she would be dead by morning.

"She really loved you, Anna," Joanne said from the doorway behind me.

I turned around and collapsed into her arms. "I know. I loved her too."

We didn't move for a long time, except for our chests, which heaved in pain against each other. Eventually, when the tears were gone, I unlatched from her. I wiped the tears from my eyes and gave her the smallest of smiles.

"Come downstairs," Joanne said. "I can't do this alone."

"In a minute," I replied.

I wanted to help Joanne, but crowds…I didn't like crowds, and I didn't like when they fawned over a girl they barely knew. More so, I hated the fact that they were all still alive and Katie wasn't. It was a horrible thought, but I just wanted my friend back. Seeing all of them alive, smiling, and being with the ones they loved, was too much for me to take.

I sat down on Katie's bed and fell onto her pillow. I could smell her shampoo. The sweet smell of roses and vanilla filled my nostrils, and for a moment Katie was alive again in my memory. I thought the tears were gone, but I was wrong. My body convulsed again, and they came back harder than ever.

Why? Katie. Why did you leave me?

It was a selfish thought, but it was a true one. I wept for Katie, for all the potential she lost, and all the days she would no longer have, but in that moment, I wept because I would never see her again. I wept because of what her death did to me.

I once had three people I loved in this world. My mother, Joanne, and Katie. Now I only had two. And I didn't love them as much as I loved Katie.

Chapter 3

I didn't want to sleep in my room any more. My room faced Katie's, across the street, and that meant memories of her flooded into my brain every time I looked out my window. I had taken to sleeping on the couch in the living room, and only sleeping with Netflix blaring *Parks and Rec* on repeat. Otherwise, the dark thoughts infested my brain.

Why couldn't you save her?

Why didn't you die?

What makes you so special?

These questions filled my brain, and I couldn't answer them. I had no idea why Katie couldn't be saved, and why I was alive while so many people I loved died.

Was I the toxic piece that killed everything around me? Was I a mold, or a spore, that infected those I cared about? Or was I just unlucky that my love was met by death at every turn. I long ago decided never to love again, but perhaps that wasn't enough. Perhaps I needed to curtail the love I had for those still alive. Maybe it was in their best interests if I just cut off all ties and ran away.

"Move over," Mom said to me, sitting down on the couch.

"Mom," I said. "I'm trying to sleep."

"Too bad, chica," she replied. "There's a TV in your room. You can use it if you want, but this one is the family TV."

I kicked her lightly, trying to get her up, but she wasn't moving. "I have school in the morning."

"You have a bed for that, my love. Now, what are we watching?"

I sighed. "Parks and Rec, I guess."

"All right, I can dig it. Which season?"

"Three."

"Ooh, that's a good one. Before or after April and Andy's wedding?"

"I don't know," I said. "It's just background noise."

She stared at the TV for a moment. "Before, definitely before. Come on, sit up. Your bony legs are poking into my side."

I pulled my legs up and Mom fell back onto the couch. "I hate you."

She rubbed my legs gently. "No, you don't. Sometimes maybe you wish you did, but you don't."

I couldn't argue with her. There wasn't anything in the world that could make me stop loving Mom, even if she was cursed to die eventually, just like everyone else I loved. It was just a matter of time.

"You realize if I don't sleep then I won't be fresh for school tomorrow?"

"Yeah, I know," she said. "But there's nothing I can do about that, besides forklift you upstairs, and I'm afraid they won't let me take one home."

Mom had the strong hands and wide build of a warehouse worker. Lots of people made fun of her when she went to work in the warehouse after Dad died, but it was one of the few places that paid decently enough for us to keep the house they'd bought before I was born. They didn't want to hire her at first, but soon enough, she proved herself, and eventually they promoted her to warehouse manager. After a few years she might even get promoted to the day shift.

"Don't you have work?" I said.

"My boss is a real dick, but even she wouldn't make me work the night of my friend's funeral."

"Aren't you the boss though?" I asked.

"There's still the owner over me, chica," she said, then sighed. "There's always a boss over you."

"Sure, but you work the night crew. Do you think they're really up to check on you?"

"No, but I'm also very self-aware. And I'm also aware when my kid doesn't want to sleep in her own room because she doesn't want to be reminded of her friend."

"So, you're a psychologist now?" I asked.

"No, but someday, maybe."

Mom was studying psychology in community college. She hoped one day to transfer to get a four-year degree, but right now it meant she was hardly ever home between school and work. Luckily, I was very self-reliant. I had been a latchkey kid for a long time, and so she could trust me to be home alone.

I scooted back on the couch and swung my legs off it. "I can't, Mom. I can't be reminded of her."

"I know, sweetie," she replied. "We both loved her, you know."

I nodded. "I know you did. She was like a daughter to you."

"She was a daughter to me, hija, just like you're a daughter to Joanne. It's never easy to lose a daughter, or a father, or a husband. That piece of your soul, it will never come back."

"Does it get easier?" I asked. "I thought it would get easier after Daddy, but it's just as hard. It's always just as hard."

"Some days will be easier than others. This day has been brutally hard, my love. But some days will be easy, and some days you will feel guilty about how easy it becomes, and it will make you spiral."

"You are not a very good psychologist, Mom."

"I'm only in my first year. Freud wasn't Freud on day one."

"No, not until he found cocaine. That's when he became Freud."

"All right, smartypants, we can all Wikipedia. That doesn't make you smart."

"No," I replied. "The straight A's make me smart."

"That just makes you book smart, hija." Mom pulled my head close to hers and kissed my forehead. "That doesn't make you street smart, and that doesn't make you heart smart, either."

"Now you sound like a Lipitor commercial."

"Just shut up and watch your show, okay?"

I snuggled into Mom's stomach and turned to the TV. I listened to her heart beat against my ear, and it slowly lulled me off to sleep. How could I ever stop loving my mother? She knew exactly what I needed. I didn't need compassion, or pity. I just needed somebody to be there, and act like everything was normal, even when nothing was, and nothing would ever be again.

*

If you liked this, make sure to pick up *Anna and the Dark Place.*

ALSO BY RUSSELL NOHELTY

THE GODVERSE CHRONICLES
And Death Followed Behind Her
And Doom Followed Behind Her
And Ruin Followed Behind Her
And Hell Followed Behind Her
Katrina Hates the Dead
Pixie Dust

OTHER NOVEL WORK
My Father Didn't Kill Himself
Sorry for Existing
Gumshoes: The Case of Madison's Father
The Invasion Saga
The Vessel
Worst Thing in the Universe
The Marked Ones

OTHER ILLUSTRATED WORK
The Little Bird and the Little Worm
Ichabod Jones: Monster Hunter
Gherkin Boy

www.russellnohelty.com

CPSIA information can be obtained
at www.ICGtesting.com
Printed in the USA
FSHW010229120720
71959FS